ALSO FROM PAUL GRIFFIN

A *New York Times Book Review* Editors' Choice
A *People* magazine Popular Pick
A Summer 2016 Kids' Indie Next Pick
An Amazon Best Book of the Year
A *Publishers Weekly* Best of Summer Pick
Working Mother magazine's #1 Best Book of the Year So Far
A 2016 Nerdy Book Club Award Winner
An *SLJ* Great Title for Middle Graders

"*Friendship* is an absolutely beautiful, heart-expanding book. I cried, but more than that I felt this giant balloon of love for everyone. This story convinced me all over again that love and imagination are life's biggest magic. It'll make you want grab hold of everyone important to you and lick them on the nose."

—Rebecca Stead, Newbery Award–winning author
of *When You Reach Me*

"Full of pace and laughter, bruises and heart. Paul Griffin is the sort of writer you're torn between telling the whole world about and keeping all to yourself." —Markus Zusak, #1 *New York Times* bestselling author of *The Book Thief*

"When *Friendship Followed Me Home* is both a beautiful book and an honest book; it is, in fact, beautiful because it is honest. We see the pain of loss, and the glory of community. We see love in its many forms, and we witness the truth that love goes on despite all barriers. Cheer for Ben and Halley: It is kids like these who are our hope."

—Gary D. Schmidt, author of *Okay for Now*

"Some books change the way you see the world. Some change the way you breathe. This book will leave you breathless. This is Paul Griffin's best book yet—and that's really saying something."

—Patricia McCormick, author of *Sold*

"This bittersweet, well-paced book . . . left me with faith that people can feel discarded, as though everything they love will be taken from them, and still end up whole, if they are touched by love and friendship."

—*The New York Times Book Review*

★ "Entrancing, magical, tragic, and uplifting."

—*Kirkus Reviews*, starred review

★ "As in his young adult books, Griffin (*Adrift*) handles hard topics with penetrating insight and honesty, while balancing painful moments (and there are many) with levity."

—*Publishers Weekly*, starred review

★ "As funny and heartwarming as it is gut-punching . . . thoroughly engaging." —*Shelf Awareness*, starred review

★ "Although this middle grade book covers some tough topics . . . it never loses hope." —*School Library Connection*, starred review

"If you have middle schoolers who are too young to fully grasp John Green's *The Fault in Our Stars* and love dogs, give them this sweet tearjerker." —*School Library Journal*

SAVING MARTY

BY PAUL GRIFFIN

PUFFIN BOOKS

PUFFIN BOOKS
An imprint of Penguin Random House LLC
375 Hudson Street
New York, New York 10014

First published in the United States of America by Dial Books for Young Readers,
an imprint of Penguin Random House LLC, 2017
Published by Puffin Books, an imprint of Penguin Random House LLC, 2018

LIBRARY OF CONGRESS CATALOGING-IN-PUBLICATION DATA IS AVAILABLE
Puffin Books ISBN 9780399539084

Printed in the United States of America

3 5 7 9 10 8 6 4 2

Design by Jasmin Rubero
Text set in Fiesole Text

For Mom and Dad

CHORDS

FINGERS
① ② ③
④

KEEP FINGER #① HERE

C	C6	C/D	C/G

FINGERS ③ ② ①   ② ①   ③ ② ④   ③ ② ① ④

D	D/G	Em	Em/G

① ③ ②   ① ③ ④   ② ③   ② ③ ④

F	F/G	G	G/E

③ ② ①   ③ ② ① ④   ② ①   ③   ①   ③

IN "CALL MY NAME," HAMMER BETWEEN C6 AND C

IN "LORENZO" AND "STAY WITH ME," HAMMER BETWEEN G/E AND G

PART I

Fall

1. CALIFORNIA DREAMING

The day Marty came into my life started normally enough. Paloma Lee and I met up before school, in the courtyard, and strummed our guitars. This was a month into sixth grade, the first Friday of October.

Pal's guitar was covered in stickers. One was a Smurf playing a guitar. She had long, loopy black hair and shiny black eyes. Not the Smurf, Paloma. She'd sewn tiny bells to the cuffs of her jeans, and every time she tapped her foot she jingled. The wash-off tattoo on the back of her hand said *The Dream Is the Only Thing That's Real*.

If you go by that height-weight chart in the nurse's office, Pal was big for her age. If you ask me, she was perfect. Her size matched her spirit. I was big too, at least size wise. Six foot two and two hundred fifty pounds isn't even on the chart when you're eleven. Everybody kept begging me to try out for football. "Renzo, you'd be a killer," they said, but I had zero interest in killing anybody. I didn't think I'd like *getting* killed a whole bunch either.

"Lorenzo Ventura, look me in the eye," Pal said. "Why you so sad?"

"I'm not *sad*," I said. "I'm smiling, aren't I?"

"That's your liar's smile," she said.

She was right. This was the day Reggie and her piglets were being auctioned off. We took in Reggie that summer when our neighbor had to sell his farm quick, before the bank grabbed it. Reggie was pregnant, and I asked Mom if we could keep the babies. She said sure, I just had to win the lottery first, and then we'd have the money to feed them.

I picked at my guitar and tried to block out the movie running in my mind: Reggie in a truck bed packed with strangers headed for the butcher. I almost told Pal about it, but then she'd be sad too. So instead I said, "Come over later for Mavericks and tacos." *Chasing Mavericks* was our favorite movie, about this kid who dreams of surfing the raddest waves in the Pacific. It had cool music too.

"Can't," Pal said. "I promised Mrs. Nikita I'd let her streamer curl my hair and hang my picture in the window. If she doesn't start bringing in customers, she's out of business."

The wind blew road sand from last winter into my eyes. Our school was at the crossroads, where the train tracks cut up with the old cemetery road. It was one of those dusty patches where the sycamores stop and the weeds creep in. The trees were bare already, gray. Fall came early to southwest Pennsylvania.

"California, Renz," Pal said.

"California, yup."

We were going to be street musicians and camp up in the hills by the Hollywood sign. Then, when Pal got discovered, I'd be her guitar man and bodyguard, just so long as I didn't have to punch anybody. We'd surf by day and jam all night. The dream was crazy, but our friendship was real.

We met in kindergarten, in peewee folk band. Pal was four when her mom caught one of those lung infections that start out a tickle in your throat, and a week later you're dead. My dad died before I was born. Pal and I were missing half of who we were. When we were together, we were one whole person.

"Quit being sad," Pal said.

"I'm *not*."

The bell rang to start school.

"What makes a hero?" Mr. Gianelli said.

Max Hawkes raised his hand. "Can I go to the bathroom?"

"I hope so," Mr. G said. "Heroes. They're rare these days. Or are they everywhere? Mr. Ventura?"

A picture of my dad came to me. Big grin, dressed in his Army uniform. He was the real reason I wanted to visit California someday. Mom had scattered his ashes in the Pacific. They'd gone out to Malibu for their honeymoon.

"Renzo?" Mr. G said.

"Heroes are rare," I said.

The combat medics have a saying: Heroes go to heaven. They have another saying too: Don't be a hero.

The bell rang, this time to end school.

"Wait," Mr. G said. "Your mission is to write about your hero, and why she or he is such."

Everybody groaned about homework on the weekend. My mind was on Reggie's piglets, sold and scattered by now, no brothers or sisters all of a sudden, no mom. If I kept thinking about it I'd well up, so I didn't, and I didn't.

2. THE BRONZE STAR

Somebody had gotten to our sign again.

COME RIGHT ON UP!
—
MAPLE CLUTCH ORCHARD
RoTTiNeST
"~~JUICIEST~~ FREESTONE PEACHES
THIS SIDE OF THE KISHUX RIVER"
FAMILY OWNED SINCE 1925

I headed uphill to the house for nail polish remover, the one thing that made permanent marker impermanent. Bella, our black Lab, didn't greet me at the door. She was two weeks from having yet another round of puppies, and she couldn't do much more than sleep in front of the wood stove. I wanted to take her up to the arbor for some air, but she wasn't in the den. I checked my room, and she wasn't there either.

The afternoon light was orange on the wall. I stood there a second, in front of my closet door, to soak in the quiet. Then, with that hero essay for Mr. G on my mind, I opened the door.

On the top shelf was my dad's Bronze Star in a picture frame.

AWARDED TO
MARTIN ANTHONY VENTURA,
FOR VALOR

His commander wrote, *"Sergeant Ventura crawled through twenty yards of crossfire to his platoon mate PFC Rajiv Bedi, who'd been hit by a sniper. Raj told Marty to high-tail out of there, since Marty was about to become a father in three months. Apparently Marty said, 'What kind of father would I be if I left my brother out here?'"*

I had pictures too. In one he's serenading Mom with his guitar. I never saw her smile that true in real life. In another, from the honeymoon, he's on a surfboard. He was big like me, and he rode it on his belly. I could hear him going "Woohoo!"

On the next shelf was a peach jar half full of guitar picks, one for each bar or wedding Dad played. He'd written the dates on them with fine-tip marker.

He'd kept a classic CD collection, Johnny Cash, Sarah Vaughan, Bruce Springsteen, Odetta. The boombox was speckled yellow and white. Mom saw him hang a flyer on the church bulletin board and hired him to paint the barn, even though it didn't need painting. Double Pop, my grandfather, told me that one, and all the other stories too.

Then there were the letters handwritten to me, before I was born. I must have read each fifty times.

Mom's truck chugged up the driveway, and the gravel *pop-pop-popped*.

I wasn't ready to be around her sadness just yet.

I snuck out the back door and forced myself down to the barn and Reggie's empty stall to rake out the straw.

Except it wasn't empty.

Bella'd had her puppies right there in Reggie's bedding. She was licking them clean. Those spiky-haired pups climbed over each other to get at Bella's milk. I ran up to the house for Double Pop.

3. THE RUNT

Ugliest puppies ever," Mom said. "Ugh, those stripes. One of John Mason's shepherds got at her again, the giant one, I bet you."

"Keeth," I said, which was short for *killer teeth*. I'd never seen him myself, but legend was he tore the throat out of a hunter who'd wandered onto Mason's property.

"That dog is the devil made flesh," Mom said. "What can you expect when his owner is Mason?"

"He called again," Double said. Mason was the condo king, and he wanted our land for a golf course.

"Daddy, I'll die before I sell to that man."

"I told him just that too." Double's grandparents started Maple Clutch, but if it was up to him, we'd sell the place yesterday and move to the Carolinas, where your money stretched so much, you could wrap a dollar around a tree, he said. Double was a soldier too, Vietnam, shot in the knee. It locked up on him in the Pennsylvania winters.

"You stay, a, *way* from that half a wolf, Renzo, and I bet

you it is one too," Mom said. "I don't want you within a mile of Mason's property. You hear me?"

"Yup."

"'*Yup.*'"

"*Yes*, okay? I understand, sheesh."

"Lorenzo Ventura, don't you *sheesh* me."

"All right now," Double said.

"Here I'm sure to be up all night with that stack of bills, robbing Peter to pay Paul, and now this mess with the dog, throwing her litter early."

"Me and Renzo, we got Bell and the pups covered."

"Striped puppies," Mom said. "I bet they don't sell for twenty dollars apiece." She marched off, but then she turned back, her eyes wet. "Sorry, Renz. I know it's not your fault."

"It's all right, Ma."

"It's *not* all right. None of it." She left fast.

"She's having a rough one tonight," I said.

"Yup," Double said, which is where I got it from. "The auction was hard on her." He patted my shoulder. His hand was a giant's but it landed on you softer than a sparrow. "I'll get the heaters and blankets, son. You break a bale and rake in some fresh straw."

I was smoothing out the bedding for the pups when I noticed one wasn't striped like the rest. He was brown and gold spots and getting stepped on by the other dogs.

Except he wasn't a dog.

He was the runt piglet Mom must have missed when she swept up Reggie and her brood for the auction.

Bella picked up that fuzzy little pig in her teeth and set him down in front of her. She looked at him, and then she looked at me.

All I could do was smile.

Bella sighed, and then she nudged that goofy-looking piglet downward so he could get his share of the milk.

Mr. Lee's police car pulled up to the barn. Pal slept over in the spare room when Mr. Lee worked the night shift, but tonight we were camping out in the barn with Bella and the pups—and the piglet.

"Is his nose red or black?" Pal said. Her hair looked pretty, streamer curled. She grabbed her guitar and rushed past me.

"You'll want your earmuffs, Pal," Mr. Lee said.

"I bet I'll survive without them, Popparoo."

"There's no telling her what to do," Mr. Lee said.

"She's doing just fine," Double said.

Mr. Lee opened the trunk. "Kindly give me a hand here, Renzo. I brought the air mattress for her, and that box of s'mores is for you, son. You said you're working on taking a few pounds off, but I figure it's Friday night, live a little. You pop 'em in the microwave, they should come out all right. Let's don't forget Miss Pal's Hug-Me-Bear in the shotgun seat. I spoil her, I know, but it makes me happy, what can I say?"

Here's what everybody else said: He was too soft to be a cop.

Mr. Lee once told me his dream was to go his whole career without ever having to draw his gun. That sounded pretty good to me.

4. MARTY

Pal lasted an hour in the barn before she headed into the house for her guestroom bed. Bella curled up next to me, and then her pups curled up next to her, the piglet too, all bunched together. The piglet slept flat on his belly with his stubby little legs spread out, like he was dreaming of flying.

I opened my notebook to get going on my hero essay for Mr. G. I'd brought along a letter from my dad.

> To My Son,
>
> Your mom tells me the doctor did the ultrasound, and now I owe her a million dollars. She swore you were going to be a boy. Apparently an angel came to her in a dream and whispered your name.
>
> Well, I don't know if I believe in angels, but I believe in your mom. If she wants to name you after her father, I can't think of a better

namesake. If angels do exist, Pop is the king of them. I guess he'll be Double Pop to you, right?

That'll be something, the four of us together at a Steelers game, or drawing in a haul from the orchard on a sunny day. We'll bunch up around that wobbly kitchen table, and after dinner we'll get the music going. I can't wait to teach you the guitar. I can't wait to meet you, Lorenzo.

Love,
Dad

I wrote and rewrote that essay, except it turned into a letter.

The piglet made snuffling noises. He was shivering. I cuddled him, and he tucked his head under my arm. He breathed in like my armpit was a perfume factory. That got me smiling big enough to show teeth.

Bella's ears went up. Double came into the barn with a thermos. "Seems you got a buddy there," he said.

He poured a cup of warmed milk for me. I dripped some into my hand, and the piglet licked it clean. His fuzzy little snout tickled me.

"How many pups we got us here?" Double said. "Ten?"

"Nine," I said.

"Unless they changed the science of counting on me, I see nine black-and-whites, plus your little gold-and-brown friend there makes ten."

"Thanks," I said, stroking the piglet's tiny ears. "For counting him, I mean."

"The way Bella's looking at you, I bet she's thinking, *Now, I don't like folks holding my pups just yet, but since it's Renzo, he can cradle the big one a minute.* He's, what now, two weeks older than the others? Two pounds heavier too. He'll get big fast."

"How long before Mom sells off the pups, you think?"

"Six weeks, I'd say, before she puts the sign out."

"Bell needs a friend, Double. Can't we keep one this time?"

"Now, you know I'd like to keep them all, son. It's just tough, you know?"

"What about him, though?" I nodded at the pig. "I don't think anybody will want him for a pet."

"No, I don't guess he's the pet pig kind. Never mind he's the runt, he'll be a good four hundred pounds by the time he's all done."

"All done," I said. I knew what he meant.

Double stroked the piglet's head. "I don't suppose you've come up with names for these here pups, have you?"

"That one with the tongue sticking out his mouth? He's Eddie."

"That's just the right one for him."

"There's Molly in the corner," I said. "Ray-Ray, Al, Bobby, Mimi, Lucy, Willow, Ziggy."

Double nodded at the piglet. "And this little fella, he doesn't get a name?"

"When you name somebody, he stays with you forever," I said.

"All the more reason to name him, no?"

The pig lapped milk from my palm. He was watching me. People say the world is a blur to a piglet at two weeks, but he definitely seemed to be taking me in. His eyes were light brown. His name came in a whisper, or I imagined it did. "Marty."

Double wiggled his hearing aid. "*Marty*, you said?"

"Double? Tell me something I don't know about my dad."

"Well, he had a smile on him, tell you what."

"You told me that a million times," I said.

"That smile though, Renz, it was just plain true. Like the way you're smiling now. Caught you there, didn't I?"

"I always feel like you're not telling me everything about him," I said. "You get this look, squinty, like you're trying to see something far, far away."

"I get to missing him is all," Double said.

"I know," I said, except really I didn't. I only knew him from pictures and letters, from the neck of his guitar, where his fingers had worn the fret board just right. "Do you think he'd mind, my dad? That I named a *pig* after him?"

"Nothing wrong with a pig, Renz. They're smarter than dogs even. I read it in a book, so there you go. Besides, anybody can see that the way you mean it, it's to honor him, your pop. The proudest moment of my life? When you were named after me." He messed up my already messed-up hair. "Boy, the way that piglet's looking into you? I think he's kind of imprinted on you, son."

"Imprinted?"

"When I was a boy we raised chickens. There's always the chick that looks different, the one who gets picked on or shunned. I'd hand-feed him, he'd look into my eyes as he ate. Forever after he'd shadow me. When a young one senses kindness, he'll follow it to the end of time. He'll pledge himself to it, because it feels—"

"Just plain true," I said.

"That's right, son. That's how it is for little Marty here. Sure, he may remember you from last week when you were checking in on Reggie, but it's different now. His family's gone, and he's a bit lost, trying to fit in. He's looking for a best friend, and he's chosen you—look at him there."

Marty rested his head on my chest. His little tail flicked back and forth. It occurred to me, why I loved animals so much: They don't know how to lie.

Already I knew how bad it would hurt, the day he'd take

that last walk up the ramp into Mom's truck for the auction.

"I'm not letting myself get attached to him, though," I said. "I'm not. I swear it."

"You swear what?" Pal said. She came in with her blanket tied over her shoulders into a cape, like a superhero.

5. DOOT-DOOT-DOO

Pal plunked down and stole Marty from me. "Oh, quit grumbling, Bella. I want him so bad, Renz, I might die."

I'd have given him to her too, to save him from the butcher, but they didn't let you keep farm animals where Pal lived, in The Tract, where the lots were small.

"I got a new song I want to try on him," Pal said. "Look out, he's nibbling the button off my shirt."

I scratched behind his ears. "Easy now, Marty."

"You named him *Marty*?" Pal said. "Does Mom know?" She'd been calling my mom hers since the day they met.

"Let's hear this song you dreamed up," Double said.

Pal handed me Marty and took up her guitar. She strummed a rockabilly pace and sang:

> Lorenzo rides into the town
> Somethin' bad is goin' down
> *Bom-ba-bom-ba-bom*

Bom-ba-bom-ba-bom

Bom-ba-bom-ba-bom-bom

Doot-doot-doo

That John Mason unleashed Keeth

Old man laughs as we all flee

Bom-ba-bom-ba-bom

Bom-ba-bom-ba-bom

Bom-ba-bom-ba-bom-bom

Doot-doot-doo

Hey *Renzo,*

You're our last hope now

Hey Renzo,

Please don't say nope now

No, no, no-no no-no Renz don't go!

Ha-ha-ha-ha-hee

Hee-he-ha-he-ho

Ho-ho-ho-he-ho-*hey*

Hey-hey-hey

Marty stared at her wide-eyed. He sniffed at her and made squeaky sounds. His tail flicked a little faster than Pal's strumming.

Renzo always brings the sun

Oh Keeth and Mason better run

Double hooted and clapped and sang along, and finally I joined in.

> *Bom*-ba-bom-ba-bom
> *Bom*-ba-bom-ba-bom
> *Bom*-ba-bom-ba-bom-*bom*
> Doot-doot-*doooooo* . . .

Bella's tail beat the straw, and little Marty stretched upward to lick my neck. Pal hummed the song to its finish, and I felt the vibration in Marty. He groaned happy as a dog lying in a sun slant, and you're scratching that mutt's belly, and everything's all right.

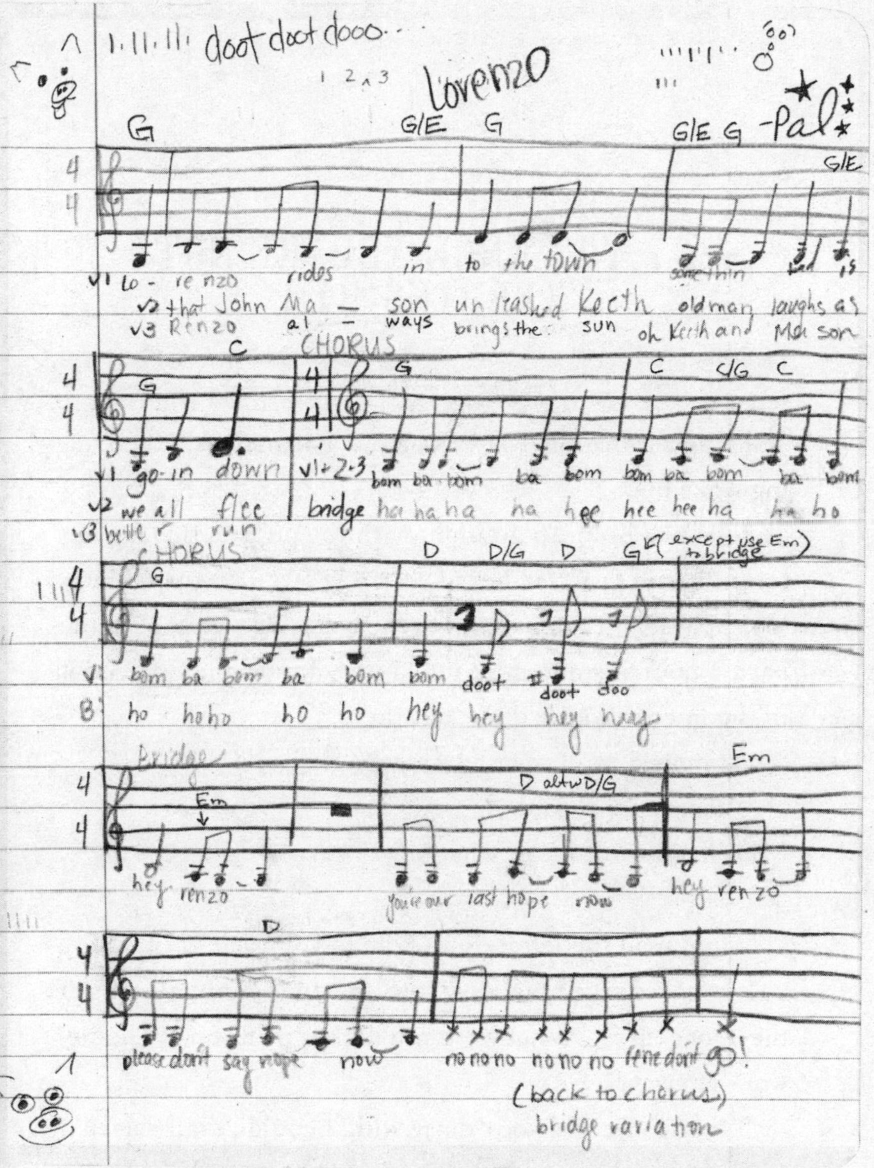

6. YOU KNOW YOU'RE NOT KEEPING HIM

The next morning, Marty was my alarm clock. His oinking woke me.

Bella had been up all night with the pups bothering her for milk, and I wanted her to get some rest. I scooped Marty to my chest and carried him to the box fridge we kept in the barn. I poured some milk into a baby bottle and warmed it in the microwave we'd put out there.

Pal moped in. "I messed up," she said.

"What now?" I said.

"What do you mean what *now*?"

"Well?"

"Mom read the letter you wrote to your dad."

I'd tucked my notebook into the tool cubby. It wasn't there, of course. "What were you doing spying on my homework anyway?"

"I thought it was your diary, duh. I couldn't fall asleep. I needed something to read. All you people have in the house

22

are those tractor mower catalogs. The midnight milk and cookies attack got me, and I forgot I left the notebook on the kitchen table, I guess. Mom said come get you."

I headed out with Marty cradled to my chest. "You *know* she always checks my homework."

"Then she would've seen it anyway. You ever think maybe you *wanted* her to see it? It was a beautiful letter, Renz, even if it is going to get you killed."

"So you just had to name that pig *Marty*," Mom said. She pecked at her beat-up laptop, and the kitchen table wobbled. She nodded at Marty, cradled to my chest. "You know that's livestock, right? You *know* you're not keeping him."

Marty's eyes were on me as he went at that milk bottle. He burped pretty loud for a little guy.

"Lorenzo?"

"I *know*, Ma."

"Mom, please," Pal said, "you can't murder Marty, you just *can't*."

"Miss Paloma Lee, get a brush through that hair and another to your teeth while you're at it."

Pal rolled her eyes on her way out.

Mom tapped my notebook, opened to the letter I wrote my dad. "Renzo, how could you? The Army? That's your plan? *You?*"

"What do you mean, *me?*"

"You're not cut out for it. Not at *all*. You'll drive me to my grave young."

Double limped up the porch steps with a shopping bag. By the shape of it, he'd picked up a carton of eggs and a box of no-name pancake mix—half the cost, twice as delicious, he liked to say. One look at Mom's frown then mine stopped him midstride. "Uh-oh," he said.

"Now I'm running late to meet the accountant, and I'm not even dressed," Mom said to Double, like it was his fault, and then she huffed out.

"Double, you think I'm tough enough to be in the Army?" I said.

"What's this now?" he said.

I explained it all to him, and he said, "Let's see that letter."

7. DEAR DAD,

Sorry I took so long to write you back. Even now this feels a little crazy. My friend Paloma says being a little crazy is good, especially if you want to be a rock star, which I do, I guess. But stuff like that, being famous and everything, that only happens to other people. So, unless there's a miracle and I make the big time with Pal, here's my plan.

After high school, I'm heading down to the recruiting station next to John Mason's office there, and I'm signing up to be a medic. I'm going to serve my country, like you and Double and a lot of people around here did. I want to make you proud.

You said you weren't sure you believed in angels, but I have to, or at least try to, because I can't let myself think you don't exist anymore, somehow, someway. Somebody as awesome as you can't stop being. If you are watching over me, you saw I named my pig after you. Sorry about that. There's something in him that makes me think of you. The just plain true part, like Double said.

Dad, you're my hero because you were as brave as anybody could be. Plus, thank you for your guitar. I feel like I know you a little better when my fingertips are where yours were.

Sincerely, from your son,

Lorenzo Ventura

8. GUTS AND PANCAKES

It's a fine letter," Double said. "It's a just plain true letter for sure."

"But do you think I'll have the guts for it someday, the Army?"

"Son, you have the guts to do anything. You'd be a wonderful medic. You'd have a great life in California too, doing the music with Pal. You got plenty of time to sort it all. Meanwhile, enjoy being eleven. Now, I'm out of milk. Grab me a quart from the barn fridge so we can get hopping on these pancakes."

By the time I was out to the barn and back, Mom was in the kitchen, dressed for the accountant. She was crying on Double's shoulder. I held up at the door and spied out her saying, "But how, Daddy? How could he *do* that to me?"

Did she mean me and my plan to join the Army? Or was she talking about my dad?

That night I huddled with Bella, Marty and the pups as I looked over my hero assignment.

I tore the letter from my notebook and started over with an essay about a Steelers Hall of Famer, Mean Joe Greene. Turns out he was nice when I met him on his autograph line. It was old-timers' day, the father-son school trip. Double took me.

I strummed softly until the pups fell asleep. I turned my dad's guitar over to the back. He'd written in blue marker across the belly:

> You can strum me, sure,
> You can pick me too.
> But when you drum me, pure,
> My heart comes through.
> My heart is a drum.

I'd asked Mom what it meant, and I got the usual, she had no idea. Even the details of his death were fuzzy. All we knew was he'd been shot in a firefight. Not the one where he got the Bronze Star for saving Raj. It was ten weeks after that, a week before I was born.

Marty was staring at me. He wriggled out of the pack, into my lap.

Holding him was different than holding the other pups. He needed more protection. His mother had been taken from him, yes, but there was something else too, something that made me think he was going to be in for a hard time in his life, no matter how long it lasted, or how short.

9. THIS DREAM IS REAL

Friday three weeks later was warm enough to eat lunch outside. Pal tuned her guitar. "That fall festival they do in Juliette?" she said. "They're opening the microphone to newcomers. We need to get up there. This isn't any school concert where a few dead-tired parents straggle in. They get a thousand-plus serious music fans over there."

"When is it?" I said.

"Next week."

"You crazy? Playing in front of that many people? We'd need a month of rehearsals, more like two."

Richie Calvo strutted up to us. If I was the biggest kid in the grade, he was the littlest. "'Sup Renz? Heard you got puppies."

"Yup."

"Heard they got Keeth blood," he said.

"Could be."

"Save like the meanest one for me, 'kay?"

Pal sighed. "You don't have to act like you're the type of

boy who wants a mean dog, Richie. Now shoo. Renzo and I have to rehearse." She nudged my knee with hers. "I need to know you're committed. I'm talking about California, the *music*. This dream is real, no plan B for me. You with me or not?"

"Course I'm with you."

"I'm not so sure, after reading that letter to your dad. Promise we'll do the open mike in the spring then, at the cinco de mayo fair."

"I swear."

"All right then." She strummed and sang, and a crowd gathered. This girl Loretta Frietas hummed along off-key. People made fun of her because she was six feet tall and because of her smile. Her front tooth was a little chipped. She was known to trip on occasion.

I liked that Loretta smiled big even though she had a messed-up tooth. She was cool.

By the time I got home Double had started the fuzz puppets on milk bottles to give poor Bella a break. We had them penned in my room now with a baby gate. "How we doing?" I said.

Double put his magic hand to my shoulder, heavier this time.

"We lost one," I said. "Bobby, right?" He was the littlest.

"I'm sorry, son." Double had wrapped the pup in a towel.

The other pups shoved each other to get at the milk bottles, but Marty? He snuggled the pup who'd died.

"Tell you what, Double."

"Tell me what."

"This pig is special. He's got soul, know what I mean?"

"I do," he said.

I buried Bobby in the orchard. Mom was raking deadwood. When I finished she gave me her water bottle. She smoothed down my mess of hair. She was almost smiling. "You're looking more and more like him."

"Who?" I said. "Him?"

I was about to ask her how I looked like him, and why was she still so mad at him all these years later, but she turned away and got back to her deadwood.

10. GIVE ME YOUR PAW.
I MEAN HOOF.

The first day of November the pups were romping in the kitchen when Mom came in. She'd gone down to the bank to beg for a loan to help us make it through to next year's harvest.

"They give you the money?" I said.

Mom shook her head. "Must these animals roughhouse in my kitchen? That *pig*, ugh. He'll eat the linoleum off the floor. I want you to feed him double rations. The sooner we fatten him up, the sooner we get rid of him. Will you look at him now? Rolling around like a dog."

"He's copying the other ones," I said.

"He's not *another* one. He's a *pig*. I just don't know about anything anymore. A pig puppy. It's ludicrous. Surely we're at the end of the world."

The third week of November, Pal put Marty on the barn scale. "Forty-two and a half," she said. "What's slaughter weight?"

"At two fifty, Mom'll start checking the auction schedule." I scooted Marty off the scale, and he wiggled into the epic wrestling match the pups had going on.

Pal fiddled with her guitar. "I dreamed about her again last night."

"Your mom?" I said.

"We sang to each other, in color too. She wore her red dress, yellow flowers in her hair. Sometimes I think she's trying to talk to me from heaven. Isn't that crazy?"

"Nope," I said. "I bet she is."

"Seriously?"

"Yes." Some days I could convince myself that her mom and my dad were watching, still caring about us. Today wasn't one of those days, but sometimes you have to lie a little to your best friend and maybe even yourself, because not lying hurts too much.

"Mrs. Nikita's closing the salon," Pal said. "The Bread & Better's shutting down too, I hear."

"Everybody's leaving to look for jobs in the city," I said.

"California, Renz."

"California," I said.

"It's sunny all the time."

"We can surf."

"People will understand us out there," Pal said. "Understand we were born to sing, to play."

I threw a tennis ball to the far end of the barn. Maniac

33

Eddie chased it down until a mouse skittered across the crumbly cement. Eddie went for the mouse, to heck with the ball.

"Almost," Pal said.

"Wait," I said. "Watch."

Marty pounced on the ball and brought it to me. I gave him a cookie. Now all the dogs rushed me, Bella too.

"Sit," I said.

Bella sat and Marty copied.

"Paw," I said.

Bella put one up, and Marty put up a hoof.

"Marty," I said, and he leaned into my leg and wagged his tail. "What, boy? Why you looking at me that way, Marty?"

"If you ever disappeared, that pig would die of heartbreak," Pal said.

It felt good, the responsibility. He picked me to be the one who kept him safe, for a little while anyway.

"Renz, how *are* we going to save him?"

"We have time," I said, but really we didn't. Marty would weigh two fifty by summer, if not before. He cocked his head and leaned harder into me.

11. THE STRIPED ONES

On a sleety December day, Mom led two girls and their parents into the barn. Ray-Ray attacked the older girl with kisses.

"How come you got a pig mixed in with your puppies?" the younger girl said. "C'mere, piggy."

Marty trotted over and offered his hoof.

"Mom, can we take this chunky monkey pig home too?"

"I don't think he'd do so well in the apartment," she said. "Lorenzo, which would be the best pup for us?"

"Sure, son, you pick," the dad said.

I nodded at Ray-Ray, belly up in the older girl's arms. "I think *he* picked *you*."

"Those stripes are the cutest," the mom said.

"The stripes *are* quite special," Mom said. "We have to charge a premium for the striped ones, I'm sure you understand."

Marty watched as they took Ray-Ray to their car. He oinked from the gate and squealed very quietly, and I guess that's how pigs cry.

By mid-January even crazy little Eddie was adopted, and it was just Bell and Marty. He was as big as she was now.

I'd never seen Bell so sad. Marty tried to cheer her up with tricks I taught him. He did the triple rollover, and Bella whimpered. He pounced on his squirrel toy and brought it to Bella for some tug-of-war.

She slumped next to Double on the couch and sighed.

Marty dropped his head. I pulled him close and scratched his chest. He thumped his back hoof on the den floor.

"Is that pig scuffing my floors again?" Mom called from the kitchen. "You get that animal out to the barn, Renzo, or we'll be having boiled ham for dinner."

"Now, now," Double said, flipping through the Wanted ads.

"Why does she have to be like that?" I said to Double.

"What'd you say about me?" Mom yelled. "Daddy, what did Renzo say about me?"

"Ben Suarez is looking for a chainsaw," Double said. "I tune up that old Craftsman, we get fifty bucks for it."

"We're not keeping that pig past spring. Lorenzo Ventura, do you hear me?"

Double stroked Bella's forehead, but she wouldn't open her eyes. "We have to fix this poor girl so she can't have any more pups," Double said.

"Mom won't let you, I bet."

"Now what are you saying about me?"

I followed Double into the kitchen. Mom looked up from her cooking, mishmash soup made from the week's leftovers. It sounds gross but it actually tasted pretty good. Marty loved it, anyway. "I've never seen a sadder pair of conspirers," Mom said.

"I'm taking Bella to get fixed," Double said.

"You are not," Mom said.

"It's a heartbreaker for her every time she has a litter," Double said. "We don't make hardly any money on those puppies anyway, by the time we've fed 'em ten weeks."

"We cleared three hundred ten dollars this last round," Mom said. "Where are my Tums? Ugh, this *pig*, sniffing at me all the time."

I clucked my tongue, and Marty came right over. He sat and gave me a hoof. "I swear he'll be learning to bark soon," I said.

"Did that pig eat my Tums again?" Mom said.

"Marty?" I said. "Woof. Woof."

Bella *woof-woof-woofed*, and Marty *groink-groink-groinked*.

"Diabolical," Mom said. "The apocalypse came and went without anybody telling me."

"He might be the smartest pup we ever had," Double said.

"He's *not* a pup," Mom said. "He *did* eat them. Look, the

wrapper's in his shoe pile. Why *do* we let him steal our shoes anyway? You boys better hope that pig sells for good money." Mom slapped the countertop. "Daddy, I know that look. Don't you start about keeping that crazy-minded pig."

"C'mon, Renzo, let's get Bell into the truck."

"C'mon, Marty, let's go for a ride." He trotted alongside me. "I'll bring you back some Tums, Momma mia."

"Oh and that'll just make *everything* all right."

As the truck pulled out I looked back to the house and saw Mom at the kitchen sink window. Her lips were moving, but she had no phone to her ear. She was praying, and I wondered what for.

PART 2

Spring

12. PEANUT BUTTER AND THE MAGIC NOSE

By April Marty was twice Bella's size. They snuggled on the couch and watched me make peanut butter sandwiches for school. Marty drooled.

The stairs creaked.

"Marty, down," I whispered.

He hopped off the couch just before Mom rushed in. "I suppose that big fat dent in the cushions was made by the Holy Ghost," she said. She filled her to-go cup with coffee. "Must you let the *pig* lick the *spoon*? And there you go again, wiping it on the bread."

Marty stood on his hind legs to reach the counter.

"Renzo, make him get *down*. That's funny to you, huh, a counter-surfing pig? Look at you, grinning like your teeth aren't crooked."

"Down, Marty. Sit."

He sat.

"See?" I said.

"I see ham hocks," Mom said. She checked herself in the hall mirror. She had an interview at the Pizza Emporium for nightshift hostess. "Ugh, my hair now with the humidity, all wound up like a travesty of corkscrews."

"You look nice," I said.

"Don't think I don't know what you're up to, trying to flatter me into letting you keep that pig. First day of summer—"

"He's off to auction, I know, I know."

"You think I'm happy about it?" Mom said. "Lookit, I'll grant you he's smart like a dog and maybe even sweet as one too, but Renz, we need that money. Double's seventy-five with a bad knee, doing that Wal-Mart restock four days a week."

"I know."

"When he's not at the Wal he's in the orchard, and when you're not in school, you're up there with him. Still we come up short each month. Mortgage, taxes, *repairs, second* mortgage—"

"*Mom,* I'm sorry you got left with this mess, okay? I'm sorry Dad got killed and you got stuck with me."

She whip-turned from the mirror and glared at me. "*Stuck* with you? You're the reason I keep keeping on." Her face softened, and now she just looked tired. "We'll give him a couple more months with Bella, your Marty there, and then it'll be time to let him live out his purpose." She popped a Tums as she left.

Marty licked the peanut butter jar clean. "Marty," I said.

He tipped over and played dead, except his tail was still wagging.

"You won't stop until I laugh, right?" I was already laughing, and then I stopped. I didn't like the play dead trick anymore.

He followed me to the door and tried to sneak out with me. "Nope," I said, and he moped into the house. Halfway down the hill I looked back. He was at the window, watching over me.

Pal was waiting for me at the cafeteria bulletin board. She tore a flyer from it and stuck it in my face.

It was for the cinco de mayo festival, a list of attractions, the Tilt-A-Whirl and Ferris wheel, the mini pony ride, the dog race, and then the jamboree, open microphone.

"You swore," Pal said.

I nodded.

"Yo, check it out," somebody yelled. "There's a pig at the window."

"Oh boy," Pal said.

"Oh no," I said. I ran into the courtyard to stop Marty from climbing through the window. Half the cafeteria followed me. Marty put on a show, first some tail chasing, then Frisbee fetch, then his trademark triple log roll with a big wet fart thrown in. That one earned him a meatball hero. He demolished it in seconds.

Everybody was laughing. They weren't laughing *at* him either. They were with him all the way. He'd infected them with his happiness.

"He tracked you good," Pal said.

"They can smell from five miles away," Richie Calvo said. "My uncle's a pig farmer. That's a *hog* you got there, Renz. Put a tag through his ear before somebody mistakes him for feral and shoots him for his meat."

The lunch lady was coming, walkie-talkie at her mouth.

"Marty," I said, "time to run."

13. MUD

Mom paced the front yard, phone to her ear. The screen door was bent open.

"Here he is now," Mom said. "It'll never happen again, I assure you." She crossed her arms and scowled at me. "I'd haul that pig to auction *today* if I thought I'd get a fair price for him."

"It wasn't that big a deal," I said.

"You cut school. You ran when the lunch aide said stop. Max Hawkes's mother wants him tested for swine flu. Don't roll your eyes at me. You want to end up in juvenile detention? See if the Army takes you then." She hurried up the porch steps.

"Mom?"

"What?"

"Did you get the job?"

"They said it was more for a teenager, seeing as it's minimum wage."

I fixed the screen door, then I raked the wildwood leaves that blew through the orchard no matter the season. Marty wrecked every last pile.

The peach trees were another story. They hadn't blossomed yet, a bad sign. I found rot on a wilting branch.

Pal came uphill with her guitar and mine. I'd left school so fast, I'd forgotten it. I'd almost lost the truest way I could know my dad.

Pal sat back against a tree and strummed. Marty plopped his giant head at her feet as she sang:

> Every time you walk away
> Every time you walk away
> Every time you walk away
> Walk away
> Walk away
> Every time you hold me tight
> In the deepest darkest night
> Every time you hold me tight
> Hold me tight
> Hold me tight
> Every time you call my name
> It just never sounds the same
> It sounds like a dreamed-for name
> Call my name
> Call my name

"For your mom?" I said.

"*To* her. Renz, let's go to the safe place."

The safe place wasn't a place. It was a thing we did since kindergarten. I sat with her and leaned in until our foreheads touched. We closed our eyes, and we didn't have to talk. As long as Pal and I stayed best friends, we could figure out anything, even a way to save Marty.

I felt another forehead on mine, and there was Marty's muddy snout.

"Hi, peanut butter breath," Pal said.

He nipped her sleeve and nudged her toward a mud puddle.

"Oh no you don't," she said.

Marty belly-flopped into the puddle. He shook himself off, and now we were shot up with mud freckles. We chased Marty and each other with mud bombs. We were laughing so hard, I didn't hear our old tractor mower chug-a-lugging uphill until it was on top of us, practically. Double named the mower Buck, because when it wasn't conking out, it was bouncing you every which way.

Bella climbed down from the trailer bed and stretched out in a sun patch. Double had Gatorades for us. "Nothing like a mud fight to set things right," he said. "You all are smiling like you won the Powerball."

"It beats crying," Pal said, crying now. "Double, how we gonna save Marty?"

47

"I've been wondering the very same thing," he said. He threw a chewed-up tennis ball. "Go on now, Bell, get it."

Bella yawned and lay back in the grass. Marty flew downhill. He fetched the ball and dropped it at my feet.

"Most pigs would eat a tennis ball before they brought it back to you," Double said. "There's got to be a way to make money off that somehow, his fetching, and then your mom'll let him stay for sure."

"That's it," I said. "That's the way to save Marty. Watch this." I whipped the ball past a short stack of peach logs. Marty hurdled them like a horse in one of those fancy shows where they jump hay bales and zigzag through the hedges. I was hooting. "Don't you see?" I said.

They didn't.

I hunted my pockets for the cinco de mayo flyer and showed it to Double. "We're gonna race him," I said.

"Course we are," Double said. "Where we gonna race him again?"

"In the dog race."

Double squinted. "Thought you said the *dog* race there for a sec, Renz."

"Yup."

"Well, at least my hearing aid's workin'."

"Hold on," Pal said. "You want to enter *Bella* in the dog as in *D-O-G* race, right?"

"Bell won't even run to her food bowl anymore," I said.

"At top speed Marty doesn't run ten miles an hour!"

"Pal's right," Double said. "Those dogs will outrun him triple speed."

"On the straightaway," I said. "Most of the course is obstacles. More than speed you need smarts. The dogs are mostly old farm hounds out for some fun. Last year half of them didn't even finish. The one went swimming in the steeplechase water, and then it turned into a pool party, remember?"

"I don't like watching those things," Pal said, "all those drunk jerks yelling at the dogs."

"It's not *grey*hound racing," I said. "It's a goof to raise money for charity." I pointed to the flyer. "What's that say about prize money?"

Pal read, "Three thousand dollars for first place."

"That's way more than we'd get for him at auction," I said.

"It also says it's five hundred to *enter* the race. He'll end up *costing* us money."

"I can get the five hundred for us," Double said. "They're always asking at the Wal if I want overtime."

"Thanks, Double, but I got it, or most of it. With grass-cutting season coming, I'll have enough by the cinco de mayo."

"Your *college* money, you moron?" Pal said. "Mom'll kill you if you spend a dime of it."

"He's gonna *win*," I said. "I feel it." I knelt and Marty

came to me. He rested his forehead on mine.

"Renz, do me a favor," Double said. "Let me be the one to ask your mom."

"If you insist," I said.

Call my name

C/D   C   Ku   C/G   Pal
                                           C

V1   ev-ery time you walk a way ——   every time you walk
V2   ev-ery time you hold me tight ——   in the deep-est dark
                                  every time you hold
V3   ev-ery time you call my name ——   it just ne - ver sounds

C/D   C

V1   a way ——   every time you walk a way
V2   me tight ——   every time you hold me tight
    est night
V3   the same ——   it sounds like a dreamed-for name ——

C6   C   C6   C

V1   walk a way   walk a way
V2   hold me tight   hold me tight
V3   call my name   call my name

CHORDS

c   c6   C/D   C/G

Paloma   hammer   every time you hold me tight
                                 in the deep est dark as night

strawberries
nuts
scotch tape
bread or buds
cheap or gross
lettuce gross
kind trial
toenail clipper
chips salsa
straws

14. A FROG'S NETHER REGIONS INDEED

We were coming downhill from the orchard when Mom drove up. She'd brought Mrs. McGrath, our accountant.

Mom eyed Pal and me. "Mrs. McGrath, how do two smart children trip into the same mud puddle?"

There were half a dozen grocery bags in the truck bed. "Marty, I need a delivery," I said.

He opened his giant mouth, and I hung a bag on his jaw. He trotted the bag up the porch steps and came back for another. He sat at Mom's feet and offered his hoof. He wagged his tail so hard, he shimmied. He cocked his head, his slobbery tongue sticking out his mouth.

"Why, that pig thinks he's a dog," Mrs. McGrath said.

"I don't like the looks on any of your all's faces," Mom said.

Double laid out our plan.

Mrs. McGrath said, "I don't believe I've ever heard such a thing as *that* anyway. A pig in a dog race? Oh no, I don't think so."

"Mrs. McGrath," Mom said, "will you kindly tell these three lunatics we don't have five hundred dollars to be gambling away on a crackpot pig?"

"The whole fair's a fundraiser for the children's hospital," Double said. "If we lose, the money goes to the kids. And anyway, Renzo wants to put up the stake himself."

"With his *college* money? Pop, you can't expect me to let the boy throw away his savings like this? What kind of lesson is that to teach him?"

"Double, I don't suppose I should butt in here," Mrs. McGrath said, "but your all's money really is tighter than a frog's nether regions."

"A frog's nether regions indeed," Double said. "The lesson here is you do all you can to protect your friend."

"A *pig* for a *friend*," Mom said. "You might as well set fire to that five hundred dollars. Paloma Lee, earn yourself a seat at the table and start peeling those potatoes."

"You got it, Momma." Pal followed Mom and Mrs. McGrath inside with a thumbs-up to me.

"Was that a yes?" I said.

"Close enough," Double said. "You think he can do it, though, Renz? You really think Marty can win?"

He was peeing on Mom's begonias, lifting his leg just like a dog. Bella groaned.

15. CINCO DE MAYO

At sunrise I was in the kitchen toasting a waffle. The dog race was just a few hours away. After that I had to play my guitar for a thousand strangers.

I wondered if my dad ever got scared, playing for a big crowd.

Bella barked to warn me of an intruder at the side door. Marty was right behind her.

Woof-*woof*, woof-woof-*woof*!

Oink-*oink*, oink-oink-*oink*!

Pal let herself in, humming. She stole my waffle and covered it with Hershey's. "I can't wait to get up there in front of all those people," she said.

"We better get in one last practice run."

"Get your guitar then."

"No, I mean for Marty."

I'd laid out a mockup of the racecourse with bales and zigzag trails marked off with rolls of POLICE LINE DO

NOT CROSS tape Mr. Lee donated to the cause.

Marty hurdled and climbed and wove through the obstacles in record time, until he got to the last hitch, the slide. It was from a swing set I found in a dumpster near one of John Mason's construction sites.

Marty climbed the straw bale steps to the top of the slide, and then like always he sat and stared out at the mountains.

"When the time comes, he'll do it," Pal said.

"Marty, come on, boy," I said.

He wouldn't budge.

The rides spun and whirled all across the five-acre lot behind the Juliette water tower. Double and Mr. Lee came with Pal and me as we walked Marty up to the entry table. I had Marty on a leash, and people were snickering.

"And how can I help you, son?" the man at the registration desk said.

"Name's Lorenzo Ventura, and I'm racing Marty."

The man checked me off his list. "Where's the dog then?"

"Well, sir, this is Marty."

"The *pig*?"

"Yup," I said.

"Yessir," Double said, putting his hand on my shoulder and standing as tall as he could.

The man leaned back and scratched his beard. "I don't know as we ever had a pig in the dog race," he said.

"Is there any rule against it?" Pal said, dagger-eyed.

"Well, I don't believe so," the man said. "Tell you what, we had a pet coyote run once."

"There you go then," Mr. Lee said.

"We made him wear a muzzle just in case," the man said.

"Marty's more likely to lick than bite," I said.

Marty did a play bow, and then he nudged the man's hand with his snout.

"He wants you to pet him," I said.

The man did, and Marty rolled over like a dog for a belly scratch. The man smiled. "I think we might have the makings for a fun race here. I don't see any harm in letting him run. You know it's five hundred smackaroos to enter, right? Plus a hundred-dollar no-aggression deposit. I trust you when you say he's no attack dog type of pig, but if he so much as nips another contestant, you forfeit that hundred bucks, understand?"

I knew about the no-aggression rule. I wouldn't have let Marty race otherwise. "You take cash?" I said.

"Depends on if it's real or not." He rubbed the bills between his fingers. "That'll do nicely. Bring Marty to the chute over there. We'll be getting started shortly."

16 . THE LONG SLIDE DOWN

The course was on the football field. So many people crowded the fence, I couldn't see daylight between them. I waited with Marty in the chute and checked out the other dogs—the dogs, I mean. It occurred to me that nasty old Mason might enter Keeth for the amusement of terrifying the crowd with a bloodbath.

This bunch of pups was all tail-waggers, about thirty dogs total. Some had been entered for a joke. How's a stub-leg Dachshund going to outrun a Great Dane? The laughing was louder than the cheering. Then I realized, everybody was laughing at Marty.

I kneeled at his side and whispered, "No matter what happens, boy, I'm so proud of you."

He licked me upside my face.

The bell rang and the gates opened.

Those dogs left Marty in the dust.

People wolf-howled and jeered him, but he kept to his business. He ran hard as he could for the first bridge where two dogs had stopped to sniff each other's butt. Another stopped to lap puddle water. Marty trotted past them, over the bridge, into the funnel tube, which scared away another dog.

I huffed and puffed to keep pace alongside Marty as he approached the traffic cones. The officials disqualified three more dogs there. One skipped the cones entirely. Another got into a wrestling match with a cone. Another stopped for a wiggly back scratch in the grass. But not Marty.

He trotted through the cones, head high, eyes front. By now people were on his side, and it was like that Rocky movie, except they were chanting, "Mar-ty, Mar-ty, Mar-ty!"

Another dog went after a chipmunk.

Another jumped over the fence.

Another shimmied under the one-foot hurdle when he was supposed to go over it—you're outta there! Marty cleared it with a dainty hop.

So it went toward the slide. It was from the fun house, a long wavy ramp. The dogs were in no hurry to go down. They sunned themselves on the deck at the top of the slide.

Marty climbed the hay bales to the top. He sat and looked out over the fairgrounds and wagged his tail. I screamed, "Come on, Marty! C'mon boy!"

"Mar-ty! Mar-ty!"

I pointed to the finish line, where people waited with treats. "Marty, cookie!"

He dropped to his belly and slid down. His bulk stopped him just short of the end of the slide. He shook himself off and trotted toward the final straightaway.

Now that they saw the slide wasn't the end of the world, five dogs scrambled down it. Four flew past Marty for the finish line. The fifth, a floppy-eared hound, wanted Marty to play with him. He looped circles around Marty like a satellite. Marty kept going—until somebody threw a bunch of hot dogs onto the final stretch.

No way was Marty going to pass that up, but neither were the four dogs in the lead. They came back for the frankfurters and hunted the grass for any they might have missed. Marty ate on the way, galloping toward the line. Now everybody was screaming his name.

My 220-pound pig was in the lead, with thirty yards to go!

Twenty . . .

Fifteen . . .

Ten . . .

The four dogs who had packed up charged past Marty and over the line.

Marty and his floppy-eared satellite were five yards from the line when the hound circled in front of him, a couple of feet shy of the finish, and then circled behind him.

Marty crossed the line, and an official draped a purple ribbon with 5's on it over that beautiful pig's neck.

I fell to my knees and hugged him. Pal kissed him, Mr. Lee slapped my back, Double was hollering I don't know what because I couldn't hear anything with all the cheering. Then one voice rang louder than the rest: "No sir, that ribbon's mine!"

He was the owner of the floppy-eared hound who'd just missed the fifth-place prize, whatever it was. "This is a *dog* race," he said. "No pigs allowed!"

He tried to take the ribbon from Marty, but the officials pushed him back. "The time to complain was before the race, not after your dog lost it," one of them said.

"If I had my rifle I'd drop that pig," the man said.

"We're having a fun time here," the head official said. "Let's all be happy about the money we raised for the hospital, Taylor."

Mr. Taylor.

I *knew* he looked familiar. The Taylors' mailbox was less than two miles down the road from Maple Clutch, but the old man was such a hermit, I hadn't seen him in years. I knew his sons, sort of. The Taylor brothers were a lot older than I was, but I'd see them hanging out in front of the liquor store, catcalling at the women who passed by.

"You stole my prize, boy," Mr. Taylor said.

"Let's go, son," Double said.

"Renzo!" Chip-tooth Loretta Frietas just about tackled me. "Thank you!" she said. "If a pig can place in a dog race, anything's possible. I'm totally going out for volleyball again. They turned me down three times already, but as the saying goes, the fourth time's a charm."

It was actually the third time's a charm, but I said, "Hey Retta? You'll make it this time, I have a good feeling." I did, too.

The mayor called me to the stage and gave me the prize Marty won, a widescreen TV.

"That one goes for $419.99 at the Wal," Double said. "They'll let me return it no receipt, take it down ten percent for the restock, add the tax back in, you're walking out of there with $400 cash money in your pocket."

"We only lost a hundred bucks!" Pal said.

"*Yesss!*" I said.

Her dad hugged us, and Double hugged some lady he didn't know, and everybody was hugging everybody.

Juliette was a rust belt town like Kishux Falls, and people were struggling—but not today. Today they had hope. They had Marty.

Out of thirty-some contenders in the dog race, he came in fifth, and he wasn't even a dog. More than that, he was the first one brave enough to take that long slide down.

He was looking up at me. His eyes caught the light, and they were gold brown.

"You did great, boy," I said. "You *are* great."

"Mar-ty, Mar-ty!"

Mr. Taylor was giving me some mean eyes, and then he turned them to Marty.

The clock tower rang three times. The public address system crackled. *"Folks, make your way to the music stage. We're opening up the mike this afternoon, with a special invitation to newcomers."*

17. PIG BOY

If the crowd liked an act, they clapped along. If they didn't, they catcalled.

You'd never know Pal had to sing in front of these thousand picky music fans in a couple minutes. She whistled and hooted and cheered the other musicians. I wanted to run away.

The stage manager came for us.

A drum roll started up. It was the blood in my ears. I couldn't remember the chords I had to play, the lyrics, the *song*.

The emcee rang a cowbell. "Please welcome Paloma Lee and Lorenzo Ventura!"

Pal whispered in his ear.

He nodded. "I meant to say the *one*, the *only*, *Miss* Paloma Lee and Lorenzo V!"

Somebody yelled, "Hey, that's the pig boy." His buddies chanted, "Pig *Boy*, Pig *Boy*!"

The audience shot back with "Mar-*ty*, Mar-*ty*!"

Marty was right up front with Double and Mr. Lee. He stared into me, tail awhirl.

I wished Mom were here to see the crowd calling his name. Saturdays she taught English as a new language in the church basement. Truth told, I never asked her to come watch me play anymore, not after I overheard her tell Double that with a guitar I looked and sounded too much like my dad.

Pal winked at me. "Renz, we're soul surfers, right?"

A soul surfer didn't care if he lost a competition, or if he won it. He surfed for the joy in it, to feel the spirit of the wave rising in his heart. My legs shook as I strummed.

Pal stepped up to the mike and said, "This one's for . . . well, you know who you are. Even if you're not here, you're *here*." She touched her heart. She sang:

> I used to walk alone
> Empty with the wind
> Hard to hold the sun
> Needing to begin
> The moon was my comp'ny
> My true nighttime friend
> Nights providing comfort
> Nights without an end, and
> I
> Love

You
I love you
Night becomes the day
Day comes like the tide
Washing all adrift
Casting all aside
Then you come to me
Why I dare not ask
Holding out a sunbeam
A chance to know my past

Everyone was stock-still, except for Pal. She swayed as
she sang with her eyes closed, the sun on her face.

Now my days and nighttimes
Both will be the same
I'll spend them all with you, calling out
I
Love
You
I love you

You've heard it said, "The crowd erupted into applause."
No, it was more like they suddenly remembered they were
alive, and they screamed to tell the world they were here.

And then it happened. Something that would happen a

lot when Pal sang in the fairs and halls and *stadiums* that would come after this one—I was sure of it. They called out to us, "Again! Encore! Again, again, again!"

We were barely offstage when Loretta Frietas rushed us. "Pal, you guys need a fan club."

"I know," Pal sighed.

Richie Calvo jumped on my back. "My boy Renzo! My *boy*!"

A woman pushed toward us. She was from the city for sure, in her slacks and high heels. "Lorenzo and Paloma—Miss Paloma, I'm Cassie Lorraine from *The Pittsburgh Jamboree*."

"Nuh-uh," I said.

"Nuh-*uh*," Pal said. The *Jamboree* was the biggest Friday night live amateur radio broadcast in the world, or at least southwestern Pennsylvania.

"Are your parents here?" Ms. Lorraine said. "You need to be on the show."

Double and Mr. Lee made their way to us. Marty wiggled himself between my legs.

"Mar-*ty*, Mar-*ty*," Cassie Lorraine said. "You're so talented, Lorenzo. An animal trainer who can play a fine guitar."

I was daring to believe that it was real after all, the dream. California.

Hollywood, Malibu, the Pacific.

We'd all be there together. Pal and me, Double and Mom, Mr. Lee and Bella . . . and Marty.

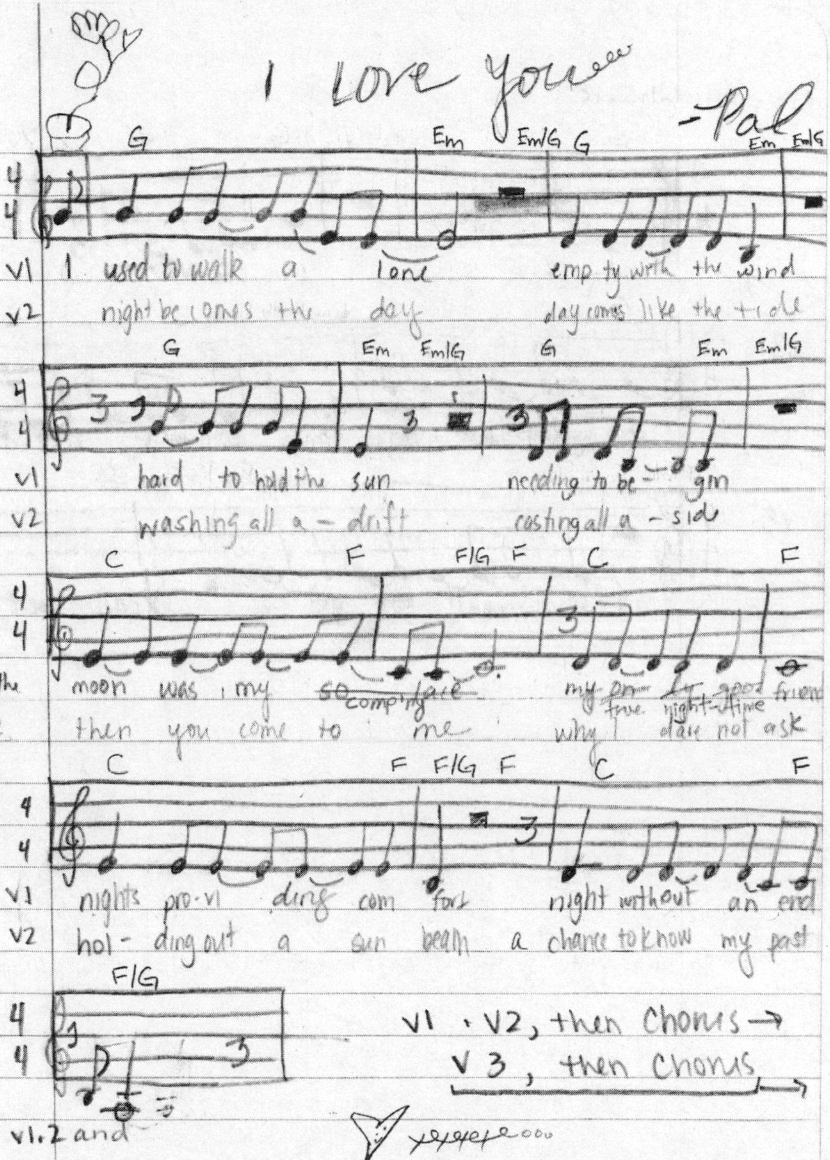

chorus
G C D D/G G C C/G D D/G D
I. love. you. I. lo ove. you.
V3
G Em Em/G Em G Em
now my days and night-times both will be the same.
V3
Em/G Em G Em Em/G Em C
i'll spend them all with you
callin' out!

18. IS HE FRIENDLY WITH STRANGERS?

The rest of the show was awesome, and then we headed for the parking lot. "You're limping, Double," Pal said. She made herself his crutch.

"*Limping?*" Double said. "I'm flying. This was one special day."

"Tell you what, it was," Mr. Lee said.

Marty nudged my pocket for his tennis ball. He liked to bounce it and catch it.

"Is he friendly with strangers?" somebody behind us said.

The Taylor brothers, one longhaired, the other shaved bald. "Congratulations," Longhair said. "Sometimes you have to tip your cap."

"Sometimes you do," one of their buddies said, except he didn't tip his cap. He wore a no-sleeves T-shirt to show everybody he spent his days in the weight room. The bunch of them were slit-eyed from too much beer. I smelled it in the wind.

The bald one—his face softened. He squatted and said, "C'mere, sweet boy."

Marty trotted to him, tail wagging, and then that Taylor kicked Marty hard enough to make him squeal.

I hugged Marty to me. I couldn't breathe, I was so mad, so paralyzed. Pal was yelling who knows what. Double and Mr. Lee held her back.

"You got a *moon* of a head on you, Pig Boy," the muscly one said. "Don't he look like a tard though? You owe Mr. Taylor a TV, melon head."

"He's twelve years old," Double said. "You're a grown man. How's about you act like it?"

They kept following us. "Him and that pig have the same size head, right?"

"Gentlemen," Mr. Lee said, "kindly stop harassing the boy—"

"Or *what*?"

"Cowardly sheriff's stepping to you, Taylor."

"Go back to China, man."

"He's Korean American, you idiot," Pal said.

"Pal, let's go," Mr. Lee said, hurrying us toward the truck.

"I may even pray for those boys tonight," Double said. "You imagine waking up and having to be them?"

I pulled down the ramp for Marty. Pal and I followed him into the truck bed. Mr. Lee flipped up the gate.

Pal was crying mad. "How could you let them talk to you

that way, Daddy? You needed to set those boys straight."

"They would have listened, you think?" Mr. Lee said. "I've learned there's a time to fight and a time to let it wash off. Now, you all did so well today, and we can't let them ruin that. You looked like your mom up there, Paloma. Like you would've been just as happy to sing if nobody was watching. You got swept up in it. You too, Renzo. It was a sight." He got into the cab with Double, and we drove off.

"You got a droopy booger in your nose," Pal said.

"Where else would I have it?" I wiped it away with my sleeve. I was so ashamed. Mr. Lee was right, about knowing when to fight. I should have stood up for Marty. If my dad was here, he'd have wasted that Taylor crew.

Pal nudged me. "Hey? We're going to Pittsburgh." She put up her knuckles for a bump, and I bumped her. Marty bumped her too, with his hoof. He leaned into me, and he was shivering as bad as I was. Soothing him soothed me. His fifth-place ribbon flapped in the highway wind, and the good feeling started to come back. There was no way Mom would make me give up Marty now, not after the way he'd shined today.

19. PUTTIN' DOWN THE OLD FOOT

Mom was at our rickety kitchen table again, papers everywhere, 60 DAYS PAST DUE, FINAL NOTICE, PAY NOW! "Well?" she said.

"He won fifth place," I said.

She looked up from her laptop.

I smiled so wide, my face hurt. I saw Double's dentures end to end too. He straightened Marty's ribbon. Marty bounced his tennis ball.

"Fifth place isn't *winning*," Mom said.

I told her about the TV, how we'd get $400 for it.

"Now *that's* a deal," she said, "spending five hundred to make four."

"I need to put down the old foot on this one," Double said.

"Before or after you get your knee fixed?"

"Marty's family."

Mom pecked at her laptop.

"Well?" Double said. "Can we keep him or not?"

"Now you're *asking*?" Mom said.

"Well—"

"Well?" She glared at Double for a second, then turned back to her papers.

"He stays then, and that's that," Double said unsurely. "C'mon, Renz. Let's wash him down in the barn. He's dusty from the wars, our porcine gladiator."

"Marty, Bell, let's go."

When we were safely outside, Double and I silent-howled. We bumped chests like morons at a Steelers game, *Touchdown!* Marty ran circles around Bella.

"Renzo, come back here!" Mom called from the kitchen.

"Uh-oh," Double said, and he beat it out of there with Bell and Marty.

I went through that door wincing. "Yup—yes?"

"One false move, and I'm hauling him to the butcher," Mom said. "And that includes peeing on my begonias."

"He'll only pee on trees from now on, I swear." I made to scoot.

"*Renzo*? How'd it go today?"

"I told ya. He got fifth."

"With the open mike, I meant. You and Pal sang, right?" *Tap-tap-tap* on that laptop.

"We did all right, Ma. We're gonna be on the *Pittsburgh Jamboree* next month."

She stopped tapping. "Why, that's something, Renz. Something big for sure."

"Mom? Maybe you could come watch us."

"Well, I, it's just so hard to get away on Fridays, with the bingo going on at the church, you know? All those old ladies, Mrs. McGrath and such, not a one of them can drive. I'll be chauffeuring them to their *funerals*."

"I understand, Mom, no problem."

"I'd be there if I could."

"Did Dad ever play live radio?" I said.

"*What?*" she said. "Why?"

"Because if he did, his guitar already got through it once. A broadcast, I mean, tens of thousands of people listening. I'm scared, Ma. Pal and I have this chance to *do* something. Something *real*, you know? What if I mess it up for her?"

"You'll be just fine. You'll be *great*."

"Sure. Thanks." I started out.

"He played live on the university station," she said.

That stopped me. The university station covered a huge area, into Ohio and West Virginia. Big stars dropped by there all the time.

"He was making a name for himself, not even trying to. That's why he was so easy to watch up there. You could tell he was playing for fun. Folks were starting to pack the bars to see him—college kids mostly. He wasn't much older than they were, but he was *older*, you know? He had gravity. The kids put him on the radio for a whole hour, primetime. Just him and his guitar. He was . . ."

"Just plain true?"

"Yes," she said. "Somebody in Detroit got wind of him— a record producer. Marty was supposed to go up there, but then things turned worse with the war, and he felt he had to, you know, go over there instead." Her voice had become so soft, I almost couldn't hear her. "That man," she said. "That *man*." She snapped to. "All right, that's enough now. Go help Double before he breaks his other knee out there in the dark."

"Mom?"

"For heaven's sake, Lorenzo, *what?*"

"Thanks. For letting Marty stay, I mean."

"Go on now," she said.

Outside, the stars were sharp and winking, and it felt like a good night for prayers. I put one up there for Loretta Frietas, that she'd make the volleyball team someday.

20. STRAWBERRIES, NUTS, STRAWBERRIES

We had four weeks until the *Pittsburgh Jamboree*. We spent three going through Pal's notebooks. She'd filled a dozen with her songs over the years, but none felt right to her. "I'd lose my mind if I could find it," she said. "I need Fro-futti."

We hiked downtown to Carmela's Confections. Pal slumped onto the bench out front with Bella while Marty tried to follow me inside. "Nuh-uh," I said.

"Oh, let him in a minute for the air-conditioning," Mrs. Carmela said.

"Thanks, Mrs. C." I got Pal her parfait and s'more swirls for me. Mrs. C gave me a bowl of vanilla too, for Marty and Bella.

They cleaned that up quick.

Pal was less happy with hers. "I wanted *strawberries-nuts-strawberries*," she said with her mouth full. "This is *nuts*-strawberries-*nuts*. You get it wrong every time."

"I'll bring it back," I said.

"I'm practically *done* with it by now anyway."

"Exactly."

"When we get rich I'm gonna have an ice cream parlor in my house," Pal said. "You?"

"Cherry-red surfboard."

Mrs. Branchinelli called to us from across the street, "Renzo, help me here a minute?" She struggled to manage her walker and a plastic shopping bag heavy with a frozen turkey—so I thought.

"Where you headed, Mrs. B?" Pal said.

"John Mason's office. Hello Bella. Marty, you're getting *big*."

"Why do you want to go to *Mason's*?" I said.

"Don't make me *talk* about it," she said, a mess of tears. "Whatever you do, don't look in that bag."

Her tabby cat was in there, dead.

"Whoa," I said.

"It was Keeth. Mrs. P's and Q's was sunning herself on the porch when that half a wolf charged from the woods. He plucked her from the stoop and shook her to bits."

"Ma'am," Pal said, "let's call my dad, and *he* can talk to Mason."

"I'm going whether you all come with me or not." She rushed her walker to the showroom window of John Mason's real estate office. I peeked between the SUPPORT OUR

TROOPS and PROUD TO HIRE VETERANS stickers on the glass, and there he was, phone in one hand, cigarette in the other, pacing. The man was a reminder to stand up straight. Cigarette fumes rose off him like the devil's mist.

Mrs. B rapped on the window.

Keeth materialized from the dimness and lunged at us. I forgot the glass was there to protect us, and I might have screamed louder than Mrs. B.

"Gah!" Pal said.

"John Mason, come out here, you horrible man!" Mrs. B said. "And you keep that Keeth inside!"

"That's not Keeth," he yelled through the glass. "That's Katrina!"

"Keep her inside too then!"

The dog snuck out with him of course. We hid behind a giant plant pot full of weeds and cigarette stubs—and no plants. Bella hid with us, but Marty wanted to play with Katrina. I latched on to his collar, and he dragged me toward the dog.

Katrina dragged Mason toward Marty. The dog snarled and gnashed.

Marty went to his belly and peed on Mason's porch.

Mason pulled a half-eaten candy bar from his pocket and threw it into his office. Katrina went after it, and Mason shut the door. He eyed Marty. "Why are you walking around with a leashed pig?" he said.

"Never mind that," Mrs. B said. "Show him, Renzo."

I opened the shopping bag.

The old buzzard peered in. He frisked his dirty jean jacket for his glasses. He looked less like an evil land baron and more like a construction worker who should have retired twenty years ago. His pants were patched at the knees.

"Why do you have a dead cat in an Applebee's bag?" he said.

Mrs. B described Keeth's treachery, the slinking and pouncing, the flying fur and blood, blood, *blood*. Meanwhile Mason hosed Marty's pee off the porch. Marty tried to slurp from the water jet until Mason squirted him in the eyes. "I'll give you three hundred dollars to walk him to the butcher for me," Mason said.

Mrs. B finished up her sermon with, "So if you can't train that Keeth to stay the hay off people's property, he'll meet my shotgun next time."

"Did the dog have a gold stripe between its eyes?" Mason said.

"How should I know?" Mrs. B said. "It all happened so fast—"

"And it wasn't at least *twice* the size of Katrina in there, was it?"

"Just about her size, I should think."

"Then it wasn't Keeth," Mason said.

"Well, it was *one* of your dozen wretched dogs," Mrs. B said.

"Didn't say it wasn't. What do you expect anyway? They're *dogs*. They *roam*." He nodded at Mrs. P's and Q's, what was left of her. "That's your housecat, you say?"

"*Was*," Mrs. B said.

"Then you ought to have kept it in the *house*. Tell you what, people like you tick me right off. Here I am bringing in construction jobs, keeping this place from turning into a ghost town, just barely, and you all come to nag me about a *cat*? And *you*," he said to me. "Keep selling grainy fruit the way you all been doing the past few years, and your mom will be begging me to buy her out. Tell her she should come to me now, while I'm still inclined to make her a generous offer."

"We'd rather starve than sell to you," I said.

"Then starve," he said.

His driver pulled up in a monster truck. Mason brushed past me, talking over his shoulder as he went. "You got a mouth on you, boy. I ought to call your daddy and—" He stopped himself. He must have remembered my father was dead and a war hero on top of that. He turned around and looked like he was about to say sorry. He didn't, but he was. I saw it in his eyes, that same squinty look Double got when he talked about my dad. "I knew him, your pop," he said, his voice quiet.

I was too stunned by his change of heart to ask him, how? *How did you know my dad?*

Tell me something I don't know about him.

Tell me why my mom grits her teeth every time I bring him up.

Mason caught himself being soft. He scowled and climbed into his truck. It shot blue fumes at us as it vroomed away.

Mrs. B dabbed her eyes with an Applebee's napkin. "I'll need help burying Mrs. P's and Q's."

"Yes, ma'am," I said. I tucked the bag under my arm.

"Don't squoosh her, now," she said.

I whistled for Bella, and she came running. "Where's Marty?" I said.

Pal pointed him out at the trash can. He was offering his hoof to a pigeon for a shake.

"That dog makes friends wherever he goes," Mrs. B said. "I wish I could be like that. That pig, I mean. That pig."

Behind Marty was the Army recruiting office. A sign hung in the window.

THERE'S STRONG . . .
AND THEN THERE'S ARMY STRONG.

21. BAD FRUIT

Sunday morning while Mom was off at church and Double was at the hospice playing cards with his war buddy, I was in the orchard with lots of fruit to pick before Pal came over for rehearsal. We still hadn't settled on a song, and the *Jamboree* was six days away.

Mason was right about the fruit. Put a slice on your tongue and it was closer to sandpaper than silk. Marty didn't mind. He gobbled every last peach I tossed him when he wasn't pestering me to throw his slimy ball. Finally he conked out next to Bella in the grass. He was four times her size now. I didn't let him sleep long in that June sun. His fur thinned on his snout, and he burned easy. I took him inside and slicked him with aloe. He kept trying to lick it off my fingers.

My hands were greasy, my arms scratched from picking. I filled the sink and cleaned up. I couldn't stop thinking about the other thing Mason said, that he knew my dad. And the *way* he said it. He was sad and something else. Disappointed?

My eyes went to the angel statue Mom kept in the windowsill.

I'd seen it a thousand times, but now it looked different. She seemed to be watching me.

I picked up the statue for a closer look. It was cheap plastic. The angel's smile was painted on crooked and a little too red.

I had a hunch now, why Mom felt so betrayed.

22. THE ANGEL

Dear Lorenzo,

Your mom will keep these letters safe for us, and when you're older, say ten years from now, we can read them together. Then you'll see the things I'm seeing over here in a world so distant from Maple Clutch, so different, so much the same. And I'll better remember this place and how it's changing me.

That's important, the remembering. It's what we build upon as we try to become who we're meant to be.

Everything I see here amazes me, and, yes, some of it scares me. The things people do to each other. The things I've done.

Better I tell you about the good. I'm still not sure I believe in the heavenly choir, but I do know an angel on earth. Her name is Hana.

She lost everything in the war. Her home,

her husband, her children. She comes to the clinic to donate blood. She travels at great risk with all the fighting going on over here. She knows we can never have enough blood on hand.

Her blood. It's all she has left, and she gives it away.

Lorenzo? Hana makes me want to believe in miracles.

23. THE SMOKESCREEN

. . . believe in miracles.'"

I'd read that letter dozens of times since Mom gave it to me a couple of years earlier, when I turned ten.

When Dad wrote, "*The things I've done,*" I always thought that meant he'd killed someone. Army medics carry guns to defend themselves. But maybe he was talking about Hana, the angel who made him want to believe in miracles.

Marty watched me. He rested his head in my lap and trembled, reading my fear.

Did my father fall in love with Hana?

My bicycle was found parts and screeched on the uphills. So did I. I was wheezing when I got to Mason's. He was known to work seven days a week.

He was there all right, on the phone, worn-out boots on his desk. I knocked on the glass. He coughed smoke when he saw me. He came to the door but didn't open it. "What now?" he said.

"It's about my dad."

He sucked his cigarette like it was a milkshake straw and breathed smoke out his nose. He opened the door and held it for me. "You comin' in or not?"

"Is the dog here?" I said.

"Which dog?"

"The one who wanted to eat my pig."

He looked around the office. "I guess not. I never know what they're up to. They're *dogs*."

"Born to roam," I said.

"Hey, that's right. Sit. You smoke?"

"I'm twelve."

"Oh. I thought you were fourteen." He took back his cigarette box. "So?"

"How'd you know him, my father?"

"He worked for me from time to time, painting apartments and such."

The cigarette fumes in there made me want to hurl. "Was he the type to be unfaithful to his wife?"

"What the hay are you talking about?" Mason said.

I showed him the letter.

He read it. "This doesn't mean anything."

"Then who is she, this Hana lady?"

"A blood donor, like it says there. How am I supposed to know?"

"You could find out," I said. "You know people."

"What people?" Mason said.

"Army people, the veterans you hire."

Mason frowned. "You about to cry?"

"No."

"Ah sheesh," Mason said. He pushed me a tissue box and lit another cigarette, and now he had two going. He *tap-tap-tapped* his phone screen. "I'm sure my buddy over there at the VA jobs program has nothing better to do on a gorgeous Sunday morning than dig up your dad's file and try to connect him to somebody named *Hana* from twelve years ago." He nodded to a model of a condominium complex spread over a table by the window. "Go look how nice all those brand-new condos are gonna be on that perfectly fine land you people are wasting on *peaches*, for goodness' sake. *Go*, and let me look into this."

The model was detailed, right down to the tiny plastic people frozen midstride in the streets. He wanted to dam the river and build a mall where it ran now. Even the hills were gone, everything just flat.

I sat back in a chair. As bad as the smoke was, the air-conditioning was nice. I hadn't slept much the past few nights or months really, and I conked out. I was too tired to dream. When I woke, the clock was forty-five minutes ahead.

"Uh-huh," Mason said into the phone. "Wait, say that again. . . . Uh-huh, that's what I thought you said. . . . Uh-huh, yup, uh-huh." He tossed the phone onto his desk.

"You find her?" I said.

"Uh-uh."

"What was all that about then? 'Say that again,' and all that?"

"Small talk." He lit a cigar now.

"Mr. Mason, you're a bad liar."

"How dare you?" he said. "Folks say I'm a *good* liar. Look, all I learned was what we already knew: Your daddy was a hero."

"Then why'd you seem disappointed in him yesterday, right before you got into your truck?"

"I'm disappointed he's not still *here*." He puffed so much smoke, I could barely see him. "Marty Ventura worked hard, no goofing off, had a nice smile too. Genuine, know what I mean? He was *honorable*. Forget about this Hana idea." Mason slapped his desktop. "You don't need to be fooling around with this stuff. It's in the past, see? Be in the *now*, or however those fruitcake hipsters say it. Be a *man*. When I was your age I didn't have any daddy around either, and look how I turned out. And I certainly wasn't lolly-gagging on a Sunday. Get a move on and go find yourself some work. Wasting half my day on a loafer. And you're welcome."

"Thanks," I said.

"Close the door behind you before you let the dog out,"

he said. "I'm just kiddin', but I like the way you jumped there."

I walked my bike down the porch steps. Maybe there was no cheater's tarnish on my dad's Bronze Star, but I wasn't any closer to uncovering the secret that fed Mom's anger all these years. Mason was right, though. Did I really want to find out my dad wasn't a hero after all? It was best to let it all lie.

I looked back over my shoulder as I rode off. The Army recruiter was peeking through the window. He nodded hi to me, and I pedaled away fast.

24. FINDERS KEEPERS

I skidded into the barn in time to meet Pal for rehearsal, except she wasn't there.

I headed for the house.

Bella was out on the porch.

The side door was open, the inside knob mangled with tooth marks.

"Marty?" I called out back. "Marty!"

Ninety degrees that day, and I was cold all over.

I rode downhill so fast, my feet came off the pedals. Pal was running up the driveway. "I was coming round the bend," she said, short of breath. "He was down the road, heading for school. I'm calling to him, chasing, he breaks into a run. This pickup U-turns, cuts him off, he cowers. Three boys jump out, haul him into the truck bed."

"Taylors?" I said.

"Plus the one with cut-off sleeves."

The Taylors' was ten minutes by bike if I didn't crash.

"Renz, wait, you can't go up there by yourself!"

The Taylors lived by the incineration plant. The air smelled like meat forgotten on the grill. Weed trees overgrew the long switchback driveway, all uphill. I'd have thrown up if my stomach wasn't empty. I followed where trucks had worn dirt stripes through the cheatgrass.

Taylor's dog howled from far away.

I followed the baying into the wildwood, until the vines were too thick for my bike. I pushed through on foot into a clearing. There was a moldy trailer and junk piled against it—car parts, tires, old office furniture, things you can sell for ten dollars here and there.

Now I understood Mr. Taylor's anger. The Taylor family needed that four-hundred-dollar TV even more than we did.

The hound's baying was louder.

Behind the trailer two men sat in broken chairs and sipped beers. "Howdy, Pig Boy," the jerk with no sleeves said. "I bet right about now you're realizing you shouldn't have come up here."

"Tommy, quit it," the other said. "You want to go to jail? Kid, I'm serious, run."

I ran all right, toward Marty's squealing. They'd tied him to a dead oak next to an antler bone tree. The dirt was greasy with blood tar.

Mr. Taylor had his butcher's knife out. Marty gnashed

like a trapped dog. The longhaired son tried to snare Marty's leg with clothesline.

"Hold him still already," Mr. Taylor said. "Poor animal is out of his mind. You want the meat to taste like fear?"

I ran head down and hit Mr. Taylor hard enough to take him off his feet. We were rolling in bramble. His sons got into the mix, and then muscle head Tommy. Mr. Taylor yelled, "Quit smacking him. Get him to your truck. Take him home."

I grabbed into the weeds so they couldn't drag me away. "I'm not leaving without my pig," I said.

"He was roadside, no tag," Mr. Taylor said. "Finders keepers. I'll send you some steaks."

I rolled onto my side and shin-kicked him.

"Ah!" The old man hopped and glared at the bald son. "Jason, get my rifle."

The Taylors' sweet old hound bounded in and licked my face. Mr. Taylor grabbed the dog by the collar. He stroked him gently and said, "Easy, boy. Go on inside now."

The dog scurried into the trailer as baldy Jason came out with a shotgun.

"Idiot," the old man said. "I said my *rifle*. We'll be chewing shot into next winter. You know what, never mind." He drew a pistol and checked the chamber. "The four of you, get that boy out of here. Go on, pick him up, an arm or leg for each. There you go. No need to rub salt in the wound by making him watch. You bring him home in one piece, Tommy, hear me?"

Tommy didn't hear too well, because he kicked me hard enough to rattle my teeth.

Mr. Taylor aimed his pistol at Marty's head. Marty squealed as they dragged me off. His squealing turned into wailing, like a siren.

It *was* a siren.

Mr. Taylor cursed a string as the police cruiser zoomed in. I swear Mr. Lee was out of that car before it stopped.

"Afternoon, gentlemen. Kindly stop roughing up Lorenzo. Step over to the car and put your hands on the roof, palms up. I'll need you to do the same, Mr. Taylor sir."

"And I'll need you to get off my property, Deputy Droopalong."

"Holster your sidearm, sir. I won't ask you twice."

"Or what, *sir?*"

Mr. Lee drew his gun. "Or I will have to shoot for center of mass."

"Center of what?" Taylor said.

"Your heart, sir, if you have one."

"Mr. Lee," I said.

"Hush now, Lorenzo. Mr. Taylor, you and your boys will put your hands on top of the cruiser there, or I will compel you to do so."

"You and what army?" Mr. Taylor said.

"Oh, they'll be along shortly," Mr. Lee said. "In fact, that's them now." The sirens whooped and squealed.

Marty and I rode home in the back of Mr. Lee's cruiser. I was shaking. Marty licked my face like I'd been pied.

"All things considered, I think we came out of that one pretty good," Mr. Lee said.

"Mr. Lee, thank you."

"Breathe, Renzo. Everything's gonna be all right. I do have to tell you though, son, back at the police academy we had a saying: Don't be a hero. You heard that one before, huh?"

"Yessir. Heroes go to heaven."

"Let's keep you here with us a long meanwhile, all right?"

I couldn't stop thinking about Mr. Taylor. That nasty man was so sweet to his dog. And land grabber Mason too—he was nice to me. It didn't make sense.

Marty nudged my hand for petting. His eyes reflected the trees and sunbreaks zipping by the window.

Mom was waiting out front when we pulled up. Mr. Lee and Pal walked away to let her give me an earful. She sort of pulled my hair too, which was her way of hugging me, I guess. And then something amazing happened.

Marty leaned into Mom's leg, and she let him. She even gave him a little scratch behind his ear.

25. CALIFORNIA (BY WAY OF PITTSBURGH), HERE WE COME

We landed on a song the midnight before the *Pittsburgh Jamboree.* "This is the one," Pal said.

"You sure?"

"I'm *so* sure."

"Good," I said. "It's the just plain truest you ever wrote."

"Renz? Thanks."

Marty nipped the cuff of Pal's jeans and stomped his hoof, which meant bedtime.

"Can Marty and Bella sleep with me tonight?" Pal said.

"Yup, and for once I'll wake up in a fart-free room."

"Not if *you* slept in it you won't."

I got my guitar ready for the next day. I changed a string that didn't feel right, then I wiped down the body with a chamois cloth to bring out the shine.

I didn't read where Dad wrote his heart was a drum. I didn't wonder about it.

I didn't let my eyes drift to my closet, didn't open the door of the shrine.

I didn't take out that old paint-speckled CD player, didn't play any Bruce Springsteen, not even my favorite, "Born to Run."

And I didn't sleep at all.

I was showered and ready to go an hour before dawn. Double was driving us up early to do a sound check. Mr. Lee was working through to noon, but he'd be there in time for the show. Mom said she tried to get out of calling the bingo, but then Mrs. McGrath got the shingles, and there simply wasn't anyone else who knew how to run it properly.

Pal and I took Marty and Bell for a walk along the orchard fence while we waited for Double. The sun was coming up through the valley.

"There it is, the glory," Pal said. She pointed to her shadow on the sparkly wet lawn. Gold light circled her shadow's head, like a halo.

"It's one of the last things I remember my mom telling me about, except she called it *la gloria* like they did in Colombia when she was a kid, she said. It happens at sunrise, sunset, when your shadow goes long and your soul is stretching out. I read about it on one of the science sites. You have to be around water, like the dew in the grass."

"Or the Pacific," I said.

Bell and Marty had glories too. I was in the shadow of a peach tree, so I had no shadow of my own. I stepped out from the shade to look for my glory when Double tooted the horn, and we had to go.

There wasn't any traffic, and we hit downtown Pittsburgh two hours early. Double took us to a diner. I wasn't hungry, but Pal put down a stack of flaps. "Renz?" she said.

"What?"

She opened her mouth wide to show me every mashed-up thing in there.

"Gross."

Double went to pay the bill and Pal went to the bathroom. She had been doodling on a notebook scrap, and I took a look.

I guess she was scared too, just a lot better at hiding her nerves. And then she came back and turned the doodle like this:

"It's on its way to being a puppy," she said. She pointed out the window. "See the cute little booger on the bench with the old man? Lorenzo Ventura?"

"Uh-huh?"

"We're gonna be awesome up there."

We said hi to the puppy, and then we took the Duquesne Incline up to Grandview Avenue. The sky was clear end to end, and the city shimmered.

I had the feeling something big was coming, like when you're in the car and your scalp tingles and a second later your favorite song comes on the radio.

The *Jamboree* people scheduled us last. All the acts before us sang fun, stomp-your-feet-type songs. Our song was quiet. I was shivering by the time the stage manager told us we were up next and brought us to the greenroom.

It was fancy, soft yellow lamps around the mirrors, velvet wallpaper, a vase full of wildflowers. Pal took a selfie and I took a minute to calm down. I'd brought one of my dad's letters and looked over the lines one last time.

Son, when you're strumming that guitar
and humming along, you're someplace else
for a while. You're in the ocean, out deep.
At first you're scared, so far from land,
but then you let the water pull on you. The

99

sky's blue like God tiled it with sapphires.
The sea, Lorenzo, it's greener than a green
M&M. And then that wave comes, the one
that catches you up, and you're on your
cherry-red surfboard, belly-riding. You
feel the water—the music—pounding back
against your broken heart, like when you
hold your guitar high during a flourish, and
the bell of it fits just right into the hollow of
your chest.

One of the girls from an earlier act came back in to get
her guitar. "Saw you two in rehearsal," she said. "I guess
you're all right."

"I saw *you* up there, and I thought you were amazing,"
Pal said.

"Yeah, I'm special that way," the girl said.

"We're all special in our own way then, right?" Pal said.

"Nope. If we're all special, then nobody's special." She
left, but not before she said, "Have fun up there, fat boy."

Pal went after her but I held her back.

"Renz, don't even think about her for a second."

"I know, I know."

"You look amazing. You *sounded* amazing in rehearsal."
She went on her tiptoes and rested her forehead on mine,
and we went to the safe place.

"You told that girl she was amazing too," I said, "even after she told us we were just all right."

"That was before I was ready to tear her hair out. Nobody messes with my Renzo."

I wondered if it really would come true, our dream. That we'd get to stay friends to the ends. We were an odd pair, if I thought about it. I spent half my life wondering about things, but Pal always knew the exact right thing to say, do, be. She was always completely herself. Pal was special.

Our names came over the dressing room speaker.

Pal leaned back and roared, "Woo-hooooo!"

26. STAY WITH ME

The stage manager rushed us down the hallway into the stage wings. There was a mess of applause and lights and the announcer saying our names and, "I'm sorry, that's Miss Paloma Lee," and then it was just the two of us onstage.

Pal said, "We dedicate this song to Marty Ventura," and my strumming hand started moving. My dad's guitar sounded beautiful up there, warm and strong. Pal sang:

> Tripped into lightness
> So true like I'm comin' home
> Love is a dancer
> Love like I've never known
> Stay
> Stay with me
> Just when I found you
> It's time that I'm gettin' on
> Wish I could linger
> Movin' on feels so wrong

Stay
Stay with me
I want you to know
You'll stay with me

I played the instrumental bridge, and Miss Paloma Lee started riffing, humming along, just letting the song pull on her. Watching her, I was flying off the top of a wave, riding the light. Pal cut back in with the final verse:

Walk on without me
Walk strong out from the shade
Know deep in my heart
My love will never fade
You'll stay
Stay with me

Nobody clapped. A few people coughed. Pal shrugged and smiled. She was in the middle of saying to me, "Sorry, Renz, I guess I messed up," when the air shook.

It stung like rain hitting you in the eyes when the wind changes too fast for you to duck behind your turned-out hand. The clapping, cheering, whistling, screaming was like the crowd was determined to knock down the building, and everybody was calling out "Paloma Lee! Paloma *Leeeee!*"

There was a minute before the people crushed in on us when Pal and I were alone behind the curtain, trying to figure out what the heck just happened. We could barely hear each other, the way the audience was going on and on.

"How do you write songs like that?" I said.

"Like what?" she said.

"You sang it like you lived it. You were telling a story about my dad, but it's like he was yours, and you knew him better than I'll ever be able to. You knew how he felt, having to leave us for the war, and then at that moment when he was dying, knowing he'd never see us again, hoping we'd be able to move on, to keep on living without him."

"Renz, it was both of us up there—"

"No, Pal, it was you. How do you *feel* like that?"

She shrugged. "It's like I know it's me out there, but I get to be somebody new for a while too. I get to surrender, to be free."

A man in a suit rushed Pal and turned her away from me so he could talk to her alone. More came with him. They swarmed her.

I headed off into the long green hallway to catch my breath.

I wasn't jealous. How could I be anything but grateful to her for letting me be with her when it happened? I'd never felt like that, a small part of something so totally dreamlike. She made the two thousand people in that theater forget their troubles for a minute. The tens of thousands listening on the radio were taken away too, I'd bet my life.

I'd had this movie in my mind of what it would be like, the first time I took off my sneakers and waded into the Pacific, the water so sparkly, greener than a green M&M. I'd be with my dad. Okay, his ashes weren't there anymore, but *he* was there.

I needed a new dream now, except I had no idea what that might be. Army medic was out of the picture too. I wasn't brave enough, at least not brave like my dad. Going up to the Taylors' to get Marty was one thing, but crawling through crossfire to save your wounded buddy? That was a very particular kind of courage. The girl in the greenroom was right: Not everybody got to be special. Heroes were very, very rare.

My face was hot. My lungs ached. I'd forgotten to breathe for how long? It was really happening: Pal was California-bound, and I wasn't going with her.

I found a bench at the end of the hall and lay back and stretched out on it. A minute later I felt her cool palm on my forehead. I opened my eyes, and there was Mom.

"Who's running the bingo?" I said.

"Who cares?" she said. "Renz? It's okay to cry."

"I'm not *crying*. They're happy tears anyway. Ma, I'm so excited for her."

"I know you are," she said.

"I mean it."

"I know you do. Hey? You were beautiful. You are."

Stay with Me

verse 1

G / G/E / G / G/E / G / G/E / G

tripped in to light ness so true like I'm com-in home

Em / Em/G / Em / Em/G / Em

love is a dan-ger love like I've ne-ver known

C / C/G / C / C/G / G

stay— stay with me

guitar (alt G and G/E)

verse 2: Just when I found you it's time that I'm gettin on.
Wish I could linger, movin on feels so wrong
Stay—, Stay with me.

G / C (alt c and C/G) / C/G / G

I want you to know you'll stay with me

G   G/E G G/E G   G/E G
3/4

~~Hope~~ you'll for- get me   walk strong out from the shade

Em   walk on with-out me Em/G   Em   Em/G Em
3/4

~~but~~ deep in my heart my love will ne- ver fade

Know   C   (alt C/G and C)   C/G   G
3/4

you'll stay   stay with me

PART 3

Summer

27. THE SCORCHER

The morning after school ended was the hottest yet, and it was time for Pal to leave.

The Pittsburgh Professional Children's School offered her a full scholarship, beginning the next September. Meanwhile, they invited her to their summer camp in the mountains. After camp, she was going to live in the city with her aunt, until Mr. Lee could find a job up there.

We strapped ourselves into the truck bed seats of Mr. Lee's pickup and headed for the train station. Bella had slept in, but Marty wasn't missing out on a truck ride. His ears and jowls flapped in the highway gusts, and that got Pal laughing, which got her crying. She yelled into the back window, "Daddy, turn around. I'm not going unless they take Renzo too."

"Oh, the drama," I said. "You think I want to go to that musty old camp anyway, singing for your supper, your lunch too, your crummy instant oatmeal breakfast?"

"You're probably right," she said. "They warned me it's rustic."

"That just means there's no free Wi-Fi."

"Promise me we'll talk every night? Serious, Renz, when I call, you better pick up."

"I always do," I said.

"*If* you're home. When are you ever going to get your own phone?"

"Never."

"You're so annoying. People want to be able to get in touch with you when *they* want."

"And that's why I don't have my own phone," I said.

Pal smoothed down Marty's floppy ears. "Marty-moo," she said.

He cocked his head and grunted.

The truck pulled into the train station. Mr. Lee made sure Pal had her Hug-Me-Bear. He hugged her fast and got back into the truck. Marty and I walked her to the platform where the train was waiting.

Now she hugged Marty. "I'll be back, boy. I'll see you soon."

He latched on to her jean cuff with his teeth.

I gave her the peach jar filled with my dad's guitar picks. "I went through them last night," I said. "Check out this one." It was close enough to gold colored, and Dad had written the name of the bar he'd used it in, Gloria's.

We touched foreheads.

The boarding bell rang.

"You're my hero," she said.

"Me? Why?"

She didn't say. She hugged me until the conductor yelled out the window, "Let's go." She went in, and she didn't look back.

Marty squealed softly, his eyes on the train as it got smaller and smaller.

"Okay, Marty, c'mon now, boy."

He wouldn't budge. I sat cross-legged next to him on the platform. He leaned into me and we stared down the empty line of track.

How in the world could I be Paloma Lee's hero? I was the guy who wasn't good enough to go to music school. I wasn't headed for anything or anywhere particularly special, I was pretty sure.

It was almost a hundred degrees that morning. It was a scorcher all right.

28. THE GROWING PROBLEM

Mr. Taylor called Mom to tell her he got sober and got religion. He wasn't asking us to drop the charges. He wanted to thank us for waking him up. So of course we dropped the charges. After that Mom hadn't seen him at church. The judge said the Taylor boys and muscle head Tommy had to keep five hundred feet away from me and my family, and that included Marty.

So I wasn't too worried about getting beat up when Mom asked me to sell peaches from our roadside table a week after Pal left for music camp. "If folks see the actual fruit, maybe they'll stop," Mom said.

They didn't.

The problem with working a slow peach stand is, you have too much time to think. If I had any chance at figuring out my future, I had to know my past, like my dad said in his letter. I kept going back to what he wrote on his guitar, *My heart is a drum*. It was eating at me. What did that mean?

Mom brought me lunch and Marty. "He keeps staring at you from the window and oinking," she said. He ate my lunch and napped at my feet.

I couldn't stop thinking about that Hana person either, the one who donated blood again and again. My dad described her as an angel on earth. Mason said Dad was honorable, not the type to fall in love with someone else besides Mom. But then again, Mason took pride in being a good liar.

Marty nudged me with his snout and put his hoof in my lap. That was his way of telling me I was wondering too much again, but I couldn't stop wondering what Pal was up to.

We talked for an hour the first night she was at camp, about how miserable she was, missing everybody. The next night we talked less, because she was tired after singing all day. The night after that, she didn't call. I got a hold of her the next night, but she was off to bed because they had an early class the next day—a *movement* class.

"Who needs somebody to teach you how to move, Marty? You just do it, right, boy? You just keep moving."

On a day this nice Pal and I would have gone tubing in the river. And then tonight we'd have watched *Chasing Mavericks* and riffed with our guitars. I hadn't picked a note since she left.

115

A month into that slow-motion summer, Marty started to get into trouble of a more serious kind.

By now he weighed three hundred and fifty pounds. He ate anything—stray grass, wild hay, acorns, all the peaches too ugly to sell. Mom's church friends dropped off slops by the pound. Feeding him was never a problem. The problem was he still thought he was a puppy.

One afternoon I came in from working the orchard. Marty jumped up to kiss me and knocked my front teeth loose. Double made a brace out of a Popsicle stick and dental floss, and I was walking around like a goof for a week while my teeth tightened into place, just as crooked as they were before too.

Another time Marty went for his ball and ran over the neighbor's mailbox. That one cost me eighty dollars for the replacement and half a day to dig a new hole and then mix the cement and set the new pole, all in ninety-four-degree heat. While I worked, Marty chased field mice. He cornered one in a weed-collecting bucket. Whether it turned on him or just had nowhere else to run but at him, Marty got scared and hid behind me, and that was the end of mouse chasing.

But it was the morning I went to cut Mrs. Branchinelli's lawn that the trouble really kicked up a notch. Marty just had to come with me, of course. When I finished up, Mrs. B wanted to treat Marty and me to Fro-fu. We were fanning ourselves on the bench out front of Mrs. Carmela's when Mrs. B and I got to debating the difference between *strawberries*-nuts-*strawberries* versus *nuts*-strawberries-*nuts*.

"How is Pal?" Mrs. B said.

I didn't know. The past couple weeks we'd barely talked once. "She's in two musicals for the summer stock," I said.

"How fun!" She slapped my knee. "Listen, let me ask you something about your Double Pop. To be perfectly frank, he is one handsome man. Do you think he might want to come over to my house for breakfast sometime?"

A little girl ran up to us. "That pig's laying in the exact same spot he was when I crossed by this way half a hour ago. Is that all he does?"

"In this heat?" I said. "Yup."

"He's ugly."

"When did children become so dreadful?" Mrs. B said. "Where is your mother at, you wretched little girl?"

"*Move*, pig!" She pulled his tail. Marty spun on her and gave her a big fat kiss. She lost her balance and plunked on her butt. She was a screamer. Her mother materialized from the air, I swear. "What happened?"

"That pig bit me!"

"On top of being an ugly little creature, your daughter's a liar," Mrs. B said.

"How *dare* you?" the mom said. She spun from Mrs. B to me. "You make us all so uncomfortable, trudging that poor hog all over creation for the world to make fun of him." She started off and then turned back. "You're just lucky Caitlin's not hurt serious. You're lucky I don't *sue* you."

"Your daughter's a deceitful little monster," Mrs. B yelled as they went off. "Poor Marty," she said, and she offered him a spoonful of her ice cream. He ate that and then the whole sundae in a bite.

Mrs. B laughed so hard she farted, and she kept right *on* farting. "Oh Renzo, I'm so sorry! Oh my, I can't stop!"

Marty stuck his nose down by her butt and breathed in deeply.

"Oh Marty, you are a *cure*," Mrs. B said, cackling. "You can't be sad around him. You just *can't*."

What the heck, I farted back at her. I *was* sad, though. What passed for entertainment these days was a fart fight with Mrs. B.

29. THE PIG-WHO-THOUGHT-HE-WAS-A-DOG DAYS OF AUGUST

In early August I got Marty onto the barn scale. "Whoa. Three seventy-three."

Marty wagged his tail like this was a *good* thing.

The mother of that tail-puller girl was right. People *were* gawking at Marty. I worried about taking him anywhere past the Maple Clutch fence these days. Still, folks stared from their cars at the pig in the dog collar—except dog collars didn't come that big. We ended up using one of Double's old Army belts.

I dumped a bucket of slops into Marty's trough. He finished in a minute and came to where I sat against the wall. He burped in my face and settled in next to me, and then we watched the heat flies zigzag past the barn door.

That night I woke up in the crack between the mattress and the wall. Marty and Bella were spread over the rest of the bed. I shoved my way back onto the mattress, and Marty grumbled. He hopped down and curled up on top of the dog bed he used to sleep in when he was a twenty-pound piglet. His belly covered the whole thing. Later he jumped back into my bed and broke it.

The legs cracked, and down we went.

That morning I woke to a rant from Mom. "A pig in a bed, and a broken one no less. I have a mind to turn him into a pig in a blanket. *Look*." She held out a peach pie, what was left of it. "I put it in the fridge specifically so he wouldn't get at it. The pig has figured out how to open the icebox door now. Marty, *bad boy!*"

Marty shivered and looked away. I swear he was thinking, *If I can't see you, then maybe you can't see me.*

"*Marty?*" Mom yelled.

He put his head under the pillow.

"Lorenzo Ventura, it's not funny."

"Then why you laughing, Ma?"

"That pie was for the church bake sale, Renzo! Goodness *gracious*, this *pig*. This poor pig. How does this end?" And now she was crying a little. She went out, and it wasn't funny anymore.

I waited until the front door slammed and the sound of her truck faded. I climbed out of my broken bed and moped to the kitchen. Double had brought home a box of Lucky Charms that'd been run over by the forklift. The manager at the Wal let him have it quarter price, which made me wonder why the forklift drivers didn't run over stuff all the time. I poured the box into two bowls, one for me, one for Marty, and then I flipped open Mom's laptop and checked Pal's Instagram.

Summer up in the mountains looked a lot more fun than summer in Maple Clutch. In one picture she was on stage dabbing with a boy as tall as I was, and a whole lot thinner. He had a ukulele strung over his shoulder. She'd already found her new backup man.

Yup, she was gone for good now.

Marty plunked his head in my lap and wagged his tail. I gave him the rest of my Lucky Charms.

The hottest day of summer came in at a hundred and three degrees, no wind. The foxtail meadow across the street was so still, it looked like an overexposed picture.

I was down at the bottom of the driveway again with Marty and the so-called peaches. This time I'd brought a moldy cocktail table umbrella to shade us. The glare was so bad with the heat wiggling off the roadtop, I had to shut my eyes. I passed out for I don't know how long.

Marty woke me with his whimpering and a nudge to my thigh, except it wasn't Marty but Bella.

"What's wrong, girl?" I looked around for Marty, and he was gone again.

Bella led me to a fresh hole in our neighbor Mrs. Tomasino's fence, then through the bramble to a small pasture Mrs. T kept for a pair of dairy cows, and right then I knew it was going to be a mess.

Back in the spring Mrs. T wanted me to bring Marty over to meet Rosie and Petunia. Marty *loved* them. They were terrified of him. They didn't mind when Bella ran circles around them and did the odd flyby, but when Marty did it? No, a pig acting like a dog was too much for a cow apparently. Marty chased them back into their barn that day, and this 103-degree day he'd chased Rosie into a gully too steep to climb out.

Marty oinked down at her from the lip of the gully. She lowed back at him. She was on her feet and grazing, but I had no idea how we were going to get her out of that ditch.

We made a blanket harness and ran a chain from it to Buck's trailer hitch. Double drove the mower while Mom and I pushed on Rosie's haunch. Bella and Marty lay down in the grass and watched.

Mrs. T thought the whole thing was pretty funny, but Mom was not amused. "I'll let you have that pig free, Mrs. T. I'll deliver him to you in the form of sausages."

"Now, Jenny, nobody got hurt, and it's all gonna be fine," Mrs. T said.

"It's not fine at all," Mom said. "Renzo, *push*, will you?"

"Ma, what do you think I'm doing?"

"Here we go," Double said. He revved Buck's engine, and there was a great groaning and then a metallic *snap* so loud, it scared Rosie right out of that gully.

"Tell you what," Double said. "That was not a particularly lovely sound."

Mom got right up into Marty's face and screamed, "Beelzebub!"

"Now, now," Double said.

"Now nothing, Daddy! Any guesses as to how much it's gonna cost to fix that tractor? Put me down for six hundred!" She popped a handful of Tums.

The next morning I was on the bowl reading the new Wimpy Kid when Mom yelled from the hall, "Renzo, mercy, can't you close the door?"

Except I couldn't. Not with Bella and Marty napping at my feet. Marty was six feet long by now, and half of him stuck out into the hall.

"When you finish up in there go help Double load the truck, and for Pete's sake if not mine will you please light a match? Do they have to be with you in the toilet even?"

"It's the only show in town right about now, Ma."

Double's war buddy had died the week before, and the man's last request was that Double head down to North Carolina to spread his ashes at Chimney Rock.

I went out to the barn to help Double get set with his

camping gear. He was with Kenny, our mechanic, who was under Buck. "You got a cracked axle here, and the struts are shot. I'd say parts and labor gonna run you close to a thousand. It's a tough one, Dub, I know."

"You don't think he can go a little longer, old Buck?" Double said. "A thousand, huh? I just don't know as we have that much on hand right now, Kenny."

"You might wring another month or two out of him," Kenny said. Double walked him to his van.

I slumped against Buck's big bald tire. Marty brought me his tennis ball, pure slobber. He bounced it and caught it. "Marty, can't you just be good?" I said. "Please, boy. *Please.*" I rested my forehead on his, and then I felt Double's hand on my shoulder, and he sat next to me. Marty tried to climb into his lap.

"Marty, no!" I shoved him away. "She's gonna make me get rid of him, isn't she?"

"We'll work it out, Renz. He's not even a year old yet. He'll calm down."

"Tell that to Mom."

"Oh I have, believe me," Double said.

"Can I see them?" I nodded at the tin container in his hand. It was exactly the size of a Coke can.

"I don't think Carlos would mind." Double screwed off the lid.

"Wow. That's really him?"

"Part of him," Double said.

He let me hold the can. It didn't look any different than fireplace ash. I don't know what I was expecting. Something more . . . Something *more*. "Double, tell me something I don't know about my dad."

"You're having a rough summer, aren't you?"

"Tell me about Hana," I said.

"Hana. Yes. Renz, I think you have a right to know everything you can about your dad, but it's not for me to tell you about Hana."

"So there is something *there*, though."

"Your mom made me promise that she should be the one to tell you, when and only when she thinks you're ready."

"I'm ready. I want to know. I don't mean to put you in the middle of it, but can't you tell me? I won't say anything to Mom."

"Now son, I wouldn't do that to your mom, and the Renzo I know wouldn't do that to his mom either. I'll talk with her after my little trip here, and we'll make time for the three of us to sit down, and your mom will answer your questions or tell you why she can't. And Renz? It's hard for her too, son."

"I know," I said.

"I know you do. Give it a few more days, 'til I get back from Chimney Rock, okay?"

"What about Marty?" I said.

"Do your best to keep him out of trouble until I'm home, and then we'll see what we can do, all right? It'll be fine, all of it."

Marty nudged my knee. He did the rollover and then took a bow. I laughed.

"*There* you go," Double said.

30. HELLO AND GOOD-BYE

Those three days Double was away were the longest of the summer and my life. I didn't let Marty out of my sight. I had him carrying peach buckets to the table stand. He lugged bag after bag of waste fruit to the mulch locker. He hauled pails and pails of water to Mom and me as we moved a bunch of baby pines from the woods down to the welcome sign, where the hose didn't reach. If it had a handle on it, Marty could carry it.

Mom hadn't said boo to me since the mess with Rosie and the ditch and most of all Buck. She'd landed a job at the Costco Lawn and Garden. Her shift didn't start until eight a.m., but she was out of the house by six to avoid me. I don't know where she went, because even the church didn't open until 7:30. But now she seemed to have cooled off a little with the weather. We were looking at low 70s and a nice breeze as the sun went down.

"Mom, please don't take him to auction."

"Put some more mulch in," she said. "Renz, I just don't

know how it ends, you know? He's gonna hurt somebody bad someday. It isn't fair to him, putting him in situations where he can get into trouble."

"So we kill him then," I said. "Yup, that'll be the best thing for him. And the fact that we'll get seven hundred dollars for his meat is beside the point."

"You don't think I know he's family now? Look at him hauling that water down here, wagging his fanny all over the place. He breaks my heart. I want him to win, you know? I *do*. I don't want him to die. I just don't know how it ends is all I'm saying." She slapped the dirt off her hands and went up to the house.

I cleaned up and grabbed the mail from the box.

I got a letter.

My heart rate doubled in a beat, because it had to be from Pal, except it wasn't.

It came without a return address or even a message, just a picture of a pig midway through the slaughter line.

After Mom went to bed I got onto her computer and tortured myself by looking at Pal's Instagram again. She posted shots of the musicals she was doing. The costumes and sets could have been from the movies, perfect lighting, cast and crew laughing away, and in the middle of it all was Pal, the star.

I *wanted* her to succeed. I just couldn't believe she'd

stopped talking to me. After all those years of being best friends, how could she forget about me so fast?

Marty put his hoof in my lap and licked me right on the mouth, but that just made everything worse, because I knew he was leaving too, and soon.

He was looking up at me the way he did when he imprinted on me or whatever it was he did that first night in the barn, when he just flat out decided we were going to be friends. From then on that pig wanted nothing more than to love me and have me love him back. The worse things got, the more he was there for me. He really was just plain true, and I couldn't figure out a way to save him.

That night I dreamed my dad was still alive. After all, there was no gravestone for him. He was off living with Hana overseas, in a city. In my dream Hana was tall and pretty, dark eyes, dark hair, with one of those smiles that made you do a double take, a *real* smile.

They had a son. He looked like me but a lot better-looking, and thin of course.

Dad just hadn't been able to make himself come back to a quiet life on a peach farm after all the things he and Hana had seen over there together. The life-or-death close calls. He had to be with somebody who'd lived with that danger and lived *through* it with him. Somebody who knew what he knew now, that every minute counted.

The dream was so real, I woke up mad. He wasn't my hero anymore. All these years he'd never wanted to know about me or even give me a call now and then. I'm not saying I needed to hear from him every night, but couldn't he have checked in on my birthday to tell me he hoped all my wishes came true, or even one of them?

But then I remembered it was only a dream. My dad died in the war. He was a hero, my hero.

But Hana was real too. Double told me as much. I had to know, what was the story with Hana?

I was at the kitchen table, Bella and Marty asleep at my feet, when Mom came down for breakfast. "I made the coffee for you," I said.

"I smelled it," she said, fixing herself a cup. "Mm, thank you, sweetheart. You look worn out. You sleep at all?"

"I don't think so. You?"

She shook her head. She sat. "So," she said.

"So?" I said.

Bella and Marty jumped and barked and groinked. Double was pulling up the driveway. I let Bell and Marty out to say hi, and I followed them to help Double with his backpack. He stepped out of the truck tanned from a couple of days in the North Carolina mountains. He held up a takeout bag from Ricky's all-night truck stop. "I got us some hushpuppies."

Marty ran up to give Double a big fat hello after three days of missing him. He tackled Double hard. Double fell back and cracked his head on the step-up to the driver's seat. He landed with a thud and then his body got still.

"Daddy?" Mom said. "Daddy!"

"Double?" I shook him and he was loose-limbed the way only a dead man can be. "Double!"

"Renzo, get that pig away from my father! Shoo, Marty! Get out of here!"

I kept shaking Double, and there was no response, just nothing.

31. DOUBLE'S KNEE

Double was almost awake by the time the ambulance came up the driveway. The EMTs took him away on a stretcher. His foot was sticking out like God put it on sideways.

I rode with him in the back of the ambulance. Mom rode up front with the driver. She was so upset, they thought it might be better to keep her away from Double, or maybe they meant to keep her away from me.

Double patted my hand and closed his eyes and said what he always said: "Don't worry, son. It'll be all right."

Two hours later Double was in a pre-surgery bed and on some medicine that made him dreamy. His knee had finally given out, and they were going to replace it. Mom paced the halls, on the phone with the insurance company or maybe her church friends. I was glad she was talking to anybody but me.

"I lucked out, huh?" Double said. "I'm gonna get a brand-new knee out of this one. Renz? I been thinking a lot about that talk we had before I left for Chimney Rock. You're going to find out about your dad sooner or later, probably sooner. I talked with your mom, and she agrees it's time you know the truth. Now, son, I want you to be ready, because it's a hard truth."

What truth isn't? I wondered.

"I want you to know that your dad will always be a hero to me. Here's why: There was a man who used to beg out front of the Wal-Mart, a vet who'd had his legs taken from him. He'd wheel up to you, stick his filthy coin cup in your face and shake it until you gave him something. By way of thanks he'd curse you, and then he'd wheel himself straight to the beer case. Oh but he was a loudmouth drunk, a profoundly angry man, I'm sure you can understand. Well, your dad was working seasonal there at the Wal, over Christmas, and he took in that poor man and got him connected with an apartment, helped him find a job too. He got him *right*, you know? Right with himself. Today he manages the nursery supply."

"Mr. Santorocco?" I said.

"Yup, and he owns part of that place now, as well."

I'd wondered why Mom didn't go straight to him for a job instead of asking around for somebody who could get her an interview with Costco, not to mention she had to drive a half hour farther to get there. But now I knew: Mr. Santorocco would only remind her of my dad.

"That's the hardest thing," Double said. "To take in the one who doesn't seem to fit in. Who needs somebody to see past what he looks like or even acts like, into the spirit. That's what your dad did for Mr. Santorocco. And son? That's what you did for Marty, and I never want you to regret it. Okay?"

"Double, I'm so sorry."

"Stop that. I'm just sad because of what he missed out on, your dad, seeing how great you turned out. Now, I don't want you to worry about anything. I'll be home in a day or two, and we'll figure all this out, I promise."

32. THE ZOO

They told us Double was going to be in surgery for a while, and maybe we should head down to the cafeteria.

We sat by the courtyard window. The glare outside made my head ache. I wasn't hungry, but I ate to keep from having to look Mom in the eye. After a long while, she said, "I forgot, Pal texted while I was on the phone with Mrs. McGrath."

"Pal?"

"She wanted me to have you call her."

Paloma Lee was pretty much the last person I wanted to talk with right then. Probably calling to tell me about ukulele boy. She'd fallen in love with him, and now her heart was broken, and she wanted good old fat Renzo's shoulder to cry on.

"I'll call her later," I said.

"Renzo, look at me. Double could have broken his neck, and then where are we with a quadriplegic in the house? Renz?"

Here it was, the verdict.

"Marty has to go. I'm just so sorry. Mrs. McGrath's cousin has a friend who owns a petting zoo up in Michigan. I sent pictures and told the people how you trained him, how he was raised in a house and loves people to bits. They want him. The say he's *ideal*. He'll be appreciated for who he is up there. He'll be safe."

"I can train him not to jump up on people—"

"Renz? No. We don't have a lot of time here, and this is the best I can come up with on short notice. I looked into some of the animal sanctuaries, but they're full, and the waitlists go on for months, and there are no guarantees he'll ever be placed. If we don't do this now, they may very well put Marty down."

"Who?" I said.

"The Animal Control people. Mr. Lee called. The hospital had to file a report with the police. Whenever an animal causes bodily injury, the authorities make a site visit. Mr. Lee says there's no way they'll let Marty stay with us in the house, not after what happened to Double. So, if they don't take him away, and we're allowed to keep him, what do we do? Put him out in the barn, all alone, no Bella to cuddle up with, no you? His heart would break. He'd forever be wondering what he did to make you hate him."

"I'll sleep in the barn with him," I said. "Mom, please."

"We're very likely going to have to sell Maple Clutch," she said. "Then what happens to Marty? Try to find a landlord who'll let us bring a four-hundred-pound pig into his building. I'm begging you, don't fight me on this. I'm just so worn out over it. At the petting zoo he'll be around other animals and kids all day. Isn't that the best plan, if not the only one?"

I couldn't match her stare.

I'd looked into the petting zoos back in the spring, before Mom said Marty could stay, when I was scrambling for any way to keep him off the auction block. The problem was, you can't put pigs into the same pen when they haven't grown up together. They'll fight to the death sometimes, I'd read. So Marty would be alone all day. And if a kid jumped the petting fence and then Marty knocked her over? They'd have to put him down for sure. I'd checked out the animal sanctuaries too, and Mom wasn't lying when she said that finding one with room for a four-hundred-pound pig could take a *long* time.

"Renz, maybe you want to go home and spend some time with him. They're coming tomorrow, the petting zoo people, to pick him up."

"Tomorrow?"

"I want to get Marty out of Maple Clutch before Animal Control comes to investigate," she said. "Go on now, okay?

I'll keep you posted about Double. The doctor told me he does ten of these operations a week, and we have nothing to worry about. You have bus money?"

"I, yeah, I think so."

"Renz, you understand it has to be this way, don't you?"

I forced myself to nod, but there was no chance I was letting Marty go to a zoo up in Michigan, where he'd never see Bella again, where he'd never see me. He *would* forever wonder what he'd done to make me send him away.

I didn't know exactly what I was going to do, but I sure knew what I *wasn't*.

"The petting zoo people," I said. "They're giving you money, right?"

"Fifteen hundred dollars, and thank the Lord. What, you want me to turn it down? I'd give them money, if I had any, if it would keep Marty safe. The way you're looking at me, Renzo, I don't know. You break my heart."

"You break mine too, lying to me all these years." I grabbed my tray and made to leave, but she snatched my arm.

"*Lying* to you?"

"About Dad. About this Hana person."

She frowned. "We'll talk about it, him, her, when the time is right."

"I've been hearing the same story from you my whole life, which is *no* story. I know what happened anyway. He didn't get killed. He ran off with Hana, and you're still jealous about it. There, you don't have to worry about telling me anymore."

"He would never do that," she said. "He wasn't that type. I can't have you think that way about him. Hey, look at me. You don't *know* him."

"And I never will, thanks to you."

"He didn't leave us for anybody else." She got hold of my hand and squeezed it. "He's gone, Renz. He's dead. He shot himself."

"Wait, say that again? Wait, don't." The cobbler I'd eaten was coming up a lot faster than I'd put it down.

33. THE TRUTH ABOUT SERGEANT MARTIN ANTHONY VENTURA

I made it outside to the courtyard trash can in time to throw up the cobbler before I choked on it. I was weak and shivering, never mind the August heat. I had to sit before I fell. The cement bench was baking hot and burned through my jeans.

My father had made all those people happy with his music. He'd saved his buddy Raj. How does that same person kill himself a week before I was born?

Now I wished he really had run off with Hana. Anything would have been better than what my mother said he'd done. It made no sense.

She was sitting with me now, wiping my chin with a napkin, rubbing my back. "Renzo, sweetheart, I know. I was the same way when I found out."

"Why?" I said. "Why'd he do it?"

"There was a last letter," she said. "The one I never gave you. I'll show it to you in a few days, after everything settles down."

"Tell me now," I said. "Tell me what he said."

"You'll need to be steady to read it. To be prepared the way I wasn't. I can't even think about it sometimes. I can't *not* think about it. We'll read it together, with Double, when he comes home. For a long time I blamed myself. There were signs after all. Warnings. My mother, on her death-bed, said, 'That man is beautiful, and he is so very *good*, but he needs watching. He's got the rain in his eyes.'"

"What's that mean?" I said.

"The sadness," my mother said. "You see it in people sometimes, even when they're smiling and making you crack up with a good story or hooting along with a song. They're thinking, *Yes, this is fun, this life. And lovely. Too lovely. But not for everybody.* For some it's so hard, the world, cold in the way it's set up. The way we all suffer through at times, on the sharp end of somebody else's greed, or our own. It's bittersweet, the living, right? I was so mad, Renz. I still am, in my more vulnerable moments. Why couldn't he come home to me for help? Didn't he trust that I would listen? That I would have stayed right along-side him, gotten him to the right doctor, the right medicine maybe?"

Her phone buzzed.

"Oh no, please Lord," she said, fishing in her back pocket. "They said he'd be in surgery another three hours."

My stomach tightened, until I saw the relief in her face.

141

"Pal again," she said. She offered me her phone. "You better call her. She's all caps and exclamation points."

"I'll call her when I get home." I took another napkin from my mother and wiped the sweat out of my eyes, except new sweat dribbled in. "I better get back to Marty and Bella. They were freaked out when we left."

"Lorenzo Ventura, can you ever forgive me? I knew I had to tell you sooner or later, but I kept thinking *let it be later*. Double said you could handle it. From the looks of you, he was right. You're strong, Renz."

"Double lied to me," I said. "He told me Dad's smile was just plain true."

"It *was*, Renz. *He* was. This is why I didn't tell you. I close my eyes and do my best to imagine being in his place, seeing the things he'd seen, doing the things he had to do. I still have trouble getting there, but it's the only way I come a little closer to understanding, to forgiving him, to forgiving myself for not being able to quit being angry with him. I work so hard to find gratitude for the time we had together. But I backslide all the time. All the time."

Now it made sense, when Mason said, *Wait, say that again*, when he was on the phone with his buddy at the VA. The friend must have pulled up my dad's file and told Mason that Sergeant Martin Anthony Ventura died by his own hand. Even John Mason, a stranger, knew about my father before I did.

"I just wish you would have told me sooner, Mom."

"When?" she said. "On your fifth birthday? Your tenth? Yesterday? Would you have been able to make sense of it then? The last twelve years, a day doesn't pass when I don't wonder about it, the same thing you'll keep wondering now. How could somebody that beautiful do something so ugly?"

Her phone buzzed with another text. She read, "'Mom, I keep trying the home phone, no luck. Do you know where he is? I'm begging you, make Renzo call me. This is a 911.'"

I took my mother's phone to a shady corner. I swear my eyes were going to pop with the glare.

34. THE (NON) EMERGENCY

Pal answered her phone on the first ring. *"Mom?"*

"Pal, it's me. What's up?"

"Renz? It doesn't sound like you."

"What's the emergency?"

"Is everything okay?" she said.

"Fine." I almost told her about Double and Marty and even my dad, but why? She couldn't fix any of it. The safe place didn't exist anymore.

"Renz, I'm in serious trouble. It's awful. I didn't get the part. The lead role for the summer finale. They gave it to this girl who's twice as stuck up as that one from the Jamboree, the one who called you fat boy. Remember?"

"Believe it or not I do."

"They have me playing second fiddle to the likes of her."

"But you still got a part, right?"

"Renz, it's like three scenes. This is my life. If I can't get the good parts in summer camp, how am I ever going to—"

"Pal? That's not serious trouble, okay? That's not even trouble."

"Wow," she said. "*Okay. So much for coming to you for a little compassion.*"

"Are you kidding?" I said. "I've been waiting night after night for you to call."

"*That's because you don't have your own phone, you stupid jerk! I can't even text you. The only way I can get you is the home phone, and I'm up at five to be on time for classes all morning, and then it's straight through with rehearsals and performances till midnight. You think I'm gonna call then and wake up Mom and Double? If you only knew what I'm going through—*"

"Well, I'll never know either, will I? It isn't always about you, okay? While you're up there in dreamland, I'm down here dealing with stuff too. Real stuff."

"*Renz, this isn't you, being mean like this. What stuff? Tell me. I never heard you so upset.*"

"Pal, I'm really sorry, but I have to go." I clicked off and brought the phone back to Mom.

"Is she okay?" she said.

I nodded. "Call me as soon as Double gets out of surgery?"

"Course." She did her best not to look worn out. She stood tall and pulled my hair a little. "That mop."

"I know," I said.

"Hey you? It'll be all right."

I was so sick of hearing that. What people really meant

was, it's rotten but you'll learn to live with it. "Mom, do I have it too? Do I have the rain in my eyes?"

She brushed my hair back from my forehead. "No," she said. "You're my sunshine."

You know how you can tell when somebody's lying to you, except maybe even they don't know they are? Like that.

35. MY HEART IS A DRUM

I saw from the driveway that Marty was waiting for me at the window. When I went into the house, Bell stayed back a little, tail between her legs. Marty crawled to me.

I pulled him into me, and then Bella too. "It's okay, you two. Everything's gonna be all right."

Now I was the liar.

They followed me into the kitchen, Marty snuffling and oinking. The floor groaned underneath him. I filled their bowls with water and poured myself a glass. I opened the freezer door and stood in front of it and let the cold fall down my back while I watched them drink.

The letter.

The last one.

The one my mother never gave me.

I went upstairs to her room, to her closet. She kept few clothes but lots of boxes full of papers about Maple Clutch, going all the way back to the beginning. Receipts and handwritten sales reports, insurance stuff. It took me an hour to go through it all, and there was no letter.

Her bookcase.

It was two shelves, and they were mostly agriculture books. I saw thin folds of paper between them here and there, church pamphlets, a half-size magazine that advertised riding mowers.

Her student Bible.

There it was, tucked into the Psalms. It was written on the same light blue paper he'd used to write me. There was a CD in there too. The label said, AN HOUR WITH MARTY VENTURA, and the university station's call sign, and the date going back fifteen years ago.

I read the letter. I don't think I breathed once the whole time I read it.

I read it again.

Again.

It was bad. It was awful. It was worse than Mom had me thinking it could be.

I wanted never to have read it. I wanted to forget it. I had to.

I balled it up and squeezed it so tight, like doing that would crush the sadness in it, the horror, until it was a small pointy stone in my palm. My legs were shaky. I sat on Mom's bed. I stared at the CD, at the Bible pages that hid the letter. My mother had underlined part of the 98th Psalm.

Let the sea resound, and everything in it,
    the world, and all who live in it.
Let the rivers clap their hands,
    let the mountains sing together for joy.

I took the CD with me. Marty and Bella were waiting for me at the bottom of the stairs. They followed me into my room, to the shrine I'd built to my father. I took out the paint-spattered CD player and put in the disc. And then I lay back on my broken bed with Marty and Bella close to me, and I listened.

Very quickly two things came to me.

First, the rain wasn't just in my father's eyes. It was in his voice too. A gentle rain, a soft sadness. In that letter he wrote about music, the magic in it, how it was like surfing, he described his heart as broken, and here it was.

Second, my father was flat-out amazing. He had that thing Pal had. Like he would sing the same way if nobody was listening. Meanwhile, he was singing to the universe.

He sang songs I'd never heard, songs he must have written, except they didn't sound written. They sounded like when you're talking with your best friend on the way home from school, and all of a sudden, out of nowhere, she says something that's so cool, you hope you'll remember it until you get to the house so you can write it down in your journal. Everyday amazing things like, *The wind has that poor bird flying sideways.*

My father sang:

> He wore secondhand boots
> of necessity, sure,
> But he didn't mind sharing
> broke-in soles, more

Or did he mean broken souls?

I'd never know.

Hearing his voice for the first time, it busted me up, because I'd never hear it again. I could listen to the CD over and over, and I would, but I'd never hear him for real. I'd never hear him say words meant only for me, like if we were at the kitchen table one night, the way he promised in his letters we would be, after dinner, just messing around with the guitar, him teaching me a new chord. He would've said, "There you go, Renz, just like that." Or "Try it this way. Feels better now, doesn't it?"

No, I'd never hear those words or any like them, only in my dreams, except I didn't think I was brave enough to dream of him anymore.

The CD ended.

I climbed over Bell and Marty to get out of bed. They followed me to the corner behind the front door, where we kept the umbrellas, where I'd left my father's guitar the day Pal went away for camp. The guitar had become dusty.

I brought it to the couch and looked over every bit of it, and it was new to me, after hearing my dad's voice. I really saw him playing it now.

I felt weird, holding it, kind of like it was a sacred thing. I didn't feel pure enough, knowing I could never play it as well as he did. Could never get my fingers quite the way he'd gotten his to tickle those notes out of that old Gibson's neck, to strum that hum up from its belly.

His hands were here.

Hands that stopped bleeding, pushed air into lungs, kept hearts pumping.

Fingers that checked pulses at the wrist, the throat.

The index finger that pulled the trigger.

I wiped the dust from the back of the guitar with my T-shirt, and I church-whispered the inscription, "'You can strum me, sure, You can pick me too. But when you drum me, pure, My heart comes through. My heart is a drum.'"

I laid my father's guitar across my knees, and I tapped the belly with my fingers, and I felt nothing. I drummed it with my palms, and then drummed harder and harder and faster, and then a lot faster and the wood started heating up. The lacquer was almost hot and my hands were going numb, and I started to hear it, this very deep tone getting caught up in the strings. They were ringing now, and twinge-ing and twanging and then buzzing, a moan rising to a howl and then, just like he promised, there it was, the music, the true heart of it, the brokenness in it, except it wasn't the guitar.

It was me.

I felt wetness on my cheek, and I opened my eyes, and there was Marty, his big old runny snout in my face. He nudged the guitar away and rested his giant head on my knee. His tail wiggled fast to shake the couch.

"Marty," I said. "What are we gonna do about you, boy?"

He looked up from where he'd buried his head in my lap. His big brown eyes were peering into me. And the thing about Marty's eyes? There was never any rain in them.

36. ANIMAL CONTROL

The phone woke me up. I forgot where I was, except how could I with Marty and Bella wedging me into a corner of the couch? How had I slept through their snoring?

"Marty." I nudged him.

He opened one eye, like a human, except his head was twice the size of mine. His tongue stuck out of his mouth.

"Let me up, boy."

He went back to sleep, and I had to shove him off to get to the phone.

Mom said Double's surgery went great. She was staying with him until it was time to tuck him in for the night. She figured she'd be back by eleven.

Eleven o'clock. I had until then to figure out a way to save Marty and be gone by the time Mom came home. The oak shadows were getting longer across the front yard.

I cursed Mom's old laptop for its slowness. I had to figure out my map, which was tricky, since there weren't any roads the way we were going.

Bella's ears went up. She ran to the front door and barked, and I heard a car coming up the driveway.

I swung the door shut and locked it. I got to Marty before he could start oinking, and I covered his eyes. That always kept him quiet. "No talking, Marty," I whispered. Blind, he still knew just where to lick my mouth with his stinky tongue.

The car tires on the gravel became louder.

No, truck tires.

Bella howled. They were rapping on the door now. The screen door swung open.

Animal Control wouldn't try to break into the house. It could only be the Taylor crew. They'd heard about Marty and Double, and now they were coming to snatch four hundred pounds of pork before Animal Control took Marty away.

I grabbed the baseball bat from the umbrella stand as the door swung open.

"Hope you don't mind that I kept my key," Pal said. "Train was packed, by the way. Had to stand until we got to Harrison. I'll stop talking. Your turn."

"Hi," I said.

"You mind putting down the bat?" She hugged me tighter than ever.

"You'll break my ribs," I said.

"I ought to, the way you were so mean to me."

Hugging her took me back to before she went away, before I learned the truth about my dad. For however long this hug lasted, I could pretend that everything really would be okay.

Mr. Lee watched us from the door. He tipped his cap and left.

37. THE PLAN, OTHERWISE KNOWN AS MY STUPIDEST IDEA YET

Pal helped me load the backpack. "Flashlight?" I said.

"Check," she said, "plus batteries, Dr Pepper, a box of Milk-Bones so huge, they have to be for a six-foot-tall dog, enough pull-tab cans of ravioli for the Boy Scout convention."

"That's a start," I said. Marty followed me around the kitchen as I raided the shelves. He knew he was coming with me, and we were headed for adventure. Bella was less enthusiastic. She eyed me from the couch like, *You sure you want to do this?*

"How are the kids up there anyway, at that camp?" I said.

"Just because they're rich doesn't make them idiots, not automatically," she said. "How about we forget *camp* for a minute, and you clue me in on the plan here."

I tapped up the website on her phone. "Heavenly Hills Animal Sanctuary," I said. "Look at those pastures. See the swimming hole?"

"There's a three-legged elephant in it!" Pal said. "It's perfect. So why all this sneaking? Mom would be happy to see Marty end up there."

"I'm sure you're right, and I bet she even tried to get him into this very one—until she found out the petting zoo would give her fifteen hundred dollars."

"Mom isn't like that," Pal said.

"I'm not taking any chances."

"Makes me sad you think that way about her."

It made me sad too.

"The bigger problem with Heavenly Hills is, it's a full house." I tapped to where the website said they weren't accepting any more animals at this time.

"Then why you showing me this place?" Pal said.

"I figured out a way to convince them to take Marty. I was reading the stories behind the animals they took in. This cat was stuck in a testing lab with electrodes poked into his head all day. The lab assistant smuggled him out one midnight, but she got caught on the security camera, and she was arrested. The Heavenly Hills people heard about her and bailed her out, and now that cat is the sanctuary housecat, even though they have a no cat rule because there are so many cat rescue places around already."

Pal was reading the story. "Aw, Mr. Pun'kins," she said. "He looks so happy now."

"I think the Heavenly Hills people will see that I'm making the same kind of effort for Marty."

"And we'll probably end up in jail too. Yes, Lorenzo Ventura, I'm coming with."

"You are so *not* coming with," I said.

"Renz, if you put up a fight over this, I'll call Mom and rat you out, and right now too. Still, here's the thing: We might need a little more than hoping Mr. Pun'kins there takes a liking to Marty enough to get the big boy through the pearly gates."

"Course we will, and that's why I'm bringing twelve hundred dollars."

"You're going to try to *bribe* your way in now?"

"It's a donation," I said.

"Course it is. Minor question here: Where we gonna get twelve hundred dollars?"

"I already got it, thanks to running my butt off for Mrs. B all summer." I patted the bulges in my pockets. "Twelve hundred and *four*, actually." I'd tried to get Mom to let me pay to fix the tractor, but she said—

"You are so *not* spending your college money on this," Pal said too. "Not after last time where she practically had a conniption after we gambled it in the dog race. I think she would have been all right losing the fifteen hundred from the petting zoo, but losing twelve hundred *college* dollars on top of that? We might as well save ourselves the trouble and check into the morgue now." She clicked up the website directions. "Looks like it's about thirty miles away. I can't call my dad for a ride. He'll never go behind Mom's back like that."

"We're not going by road," I said. "We're cutting directly across, all farmland, into the nature preserve, state land straight to the river, and then the sanctuary is just a mile east of the Kishux. Twelve miles total."

"A twelve-mile hike," Pal said, "most of it in the pitch-dark woods tonight? We'll break our ankles inside of the first mile."

"We're not hiking either."

"Pogo sticks?" Pal said.

"Buck," I said.

"*Buck?* No sir. Buckaroo'll throw us the first ditch we hit. Renz, Buck can barely cut a flat lawn without breaking down."

"And that was before his axle was messed up," I said.

"This is the stupidest idea you've had yet, and that's really saying something."

"Exactly," I said, "and that's why you should stay here."

"And face the wrath of Mom on my own?" she said. "Let's quit gabbing and get out of here before the sun sets."

"Miss Paloma Lee? Thanks for coming with."

38. BUCK

The first part of the trip was easy, because it was all Maple Clutch land, and I knew every rut and sand slide in those hills. The nature preserve wasn't bad either. The trails were wide and tamped smooth in most places, even if they were a little hard to see. The sky was clear and dry with a strong breeze, but there was no moon yet, and Buck's headlights were weak. Pal rode shotgun and aimed the flashlight ahead.

Marty thought this night ride was awesome. He grunted and groinked the whole time and leaned forward from the trailer to lick the back of my neck.

"It's sad how he and Bella didn't even get to say a proper good-bye," Pal said.

"It's better that way," I said.

"She'll be wondering where he is by tomorrow morning, and then she'll keep wondering and wondering. And Marty, he'll be wondering too, and wondering and wondering—"

"I get it, Pal."

"About *you*, I was going to say."

"I know what you meant," I said. "I don't want to think about it until I have to."

"Hey, you'll be able to see him from time to time," she said.

"That's the biggest reason I'm bringing him here."

"The trees are puffing up like hair blow-dried in slow motion," Pal said. "That's some wind."

"Yeah," I said. "Could you shine the light in front of us, so I can see where I'm driving?"

She swung the flashlight beam off the trees and put it where I needed it. "I bet they take him," she said. "The Heavenly Hills people."

"Oh, they will," I said.

"For sure."

"Yup."

"Hey, Renz? It's gonna be all right."

"I wish people would stop saying that."

"I know," she said.

"How do you do that?" I said. "How do you think up things like, 'The trees are puffing up like hair blow-dried in slow motion'?"

"Because they are," she said.

"You're sort of spectacular."

"Aw. I miss you guys."

"Yeah," I said. "You want to tell me about that part in the finale?"

"The one I got or the one I didn't?" she said.

"I feel bad, saying your problems weren't real, that mine were bigger than yours."

"Renz, your problems *are* bigger than mine. There's something else too. Something you're not telling me. Don't lie."

"I won't."

"Then cough it up," she said.

"I don't think I'm ready to talk about it yet. I don't understand it myself. You mind if we just ride quiet for a little?"

She locked her mouth with an invisible key, and then opened her mouth to swallow it.

I didn't even want to *think* about my dad, not then.

Marty rested his chin on my shoulder.

I wondered if I could still be me without him there every day. The new me, the one Marty made me into. Taking care of him, protecting him, being his whole world sometimes—I needed that. He made me feel like I had a purpose in this life.

Double's words hit me hard when he said he felt bad my dad never got to watch me grow up. I'd gotten to do that with Marty. I'd watched him go from pup to steady racer to cow chaser to workhorse, the way he got a kick out of lugging whatever you hung on his jaw.

The way he played catch with himself with that disgusting, slobbery tennis ball.

I'd miss scratching the fur on the side of his neck, his

chest. I'd feel his heart in my fingertips, in my arms, rising into my spirit. That kind of humming and buzzing is too good and true to let it pass you by without stealing a little for yourself, because what do you know, you're not sad anymore, or nervous, or mad. You're just you the way you're meant to be, feeling lucky to be here.

But I'd see him again. I would, a lot. I'd visit him every day I could get a ride out there. I bet Double would take me at least twice a week anyway. It wouldn't wear off either, wanting to spend time with him. It would stay strong in me for as long as he lived.

If the sanctuary took him.

One of the struts blew, and poor Buck bottomed out in a furrow.

"Yup," Pal said. "RIP, Buckaroo. You got us three-quarters of the way there anyhow. Renz, I think you might want to consider never going home again. For your next trick, any ideas as to how we get Marty through these last three pitch-dark miles to the Heavenly Hills?"

"Now we hike," I said.

We put fresh batteries into the flashlights and loaded up our sleeping bags and snacks and hoofed it through the nature preserve toward the Kishux River.

39. THE RIVER

Marty kept pulling over to the side of the trail every time he smelled mushrooms. He vacuumed up patches of them. "Marty, let's go."

He trotted along happily, nipping at the cuffs of my jeans to get me to chase him. "Easy, boy. We'll play stick fetch at the river."

We heard the water before we saw it on Pal's GPS, which said the Kishux was just on the other side of an evergreen thicket that had grown tall in the middle. The outline of the treetops angled steep like a cathedral roof. The pines broke into a slope of wild grass, and then we were at the riverbank.

The Kishux River was high with the summer rains. The water picked up air when it rushed over the rocks, and the froth was light green. The moon was on the rise now, and we didn't need flashlights.

Across the river was pastureland overgrown with weed trees. It had been a horse ranch. "Remember when Double took us riding there that time," I said. "When was that, first grade?"

"Second maybe," Pal said. "Where's Marty?"

I nodded toward a patch of high grass. "Peeing. I wonder what happened to them."

"Who?" Pal said.

"The horses."

"I wonder too," Pal said.

"Can you pull up Google Earth again?" I said.

She did and zoomed in on the field. There were all these metallic white mounds and then dusky ones. "What is that?" she said.

"I don't know about the white stuff, but those gray things look like piles of tires. They turned the place into an illegal dump, I bet. Yup, see all those burned-out cars? I don't think it's a good idea to cross it now."

"People hanging out maybe, getting drunk?" Pal said.

"Could be, but I'm more worried that with all the high grass and garbage and the dark, we'll run into something sharp or fall into a ditch."

"Says on the map it's three-quarters of a scary mile to the sanctuary fence," Pal said. "I wouldn't mind staying here until sunrise."

"That sounds about right," I said.

"Renz, listen. You hear it? The river's one long soft whoosh. I like this music."

We set up camp a few feet from the river's edge. As hot as it got during the August days, the nights were cold in southwest Pennsylvania. We built a rock pit and got the fatwood starter going and piled deadwood on top, and inside of ten minutes we were sweating as we cooked the ravioli right in the cans. Marty ate a box of dog biscuits and four cans of dog food.

"His burps stink," Pal said. "C'mere anyway Marty. C'mere boy." They touched foreheads and Pal whispered to him, what I don't know.

We misted each other with bug spray and laid out the sleeping bags. The owls hooted, the coyotes yipped, and Marty burrowed into my sleeping bag to hide from the sounds. I stole what bit of sleeping bag I could from him. The ground was soft, all sand. "What did you say in that note to Mom?"

"We went camping, see you tomorrow," Pal said.

"Went camping, hasta mañana—she'll love that," I said. "Your dad too."

"Yeah, we're dead. Poor Bella. Her ears will be bleeding right about now."

"You turned off your phone, right?"

"I told you I did," she said.

"I don't want anybody tracking us."

"You told me. Renz, you watch too many movies."

"I don't watch any movies since we got rid of cable."

"I'd die," Pal said.

"You wouldn't."

"You're probably right. No, you're right," she said.

"You're missing rehearsal tonight," I said. "They gonna be mad at you?"

"They understand it's a family emergency. Hey, you want to talk?"

"What do you call what we're doing now?"

"Yeah," Pal said, "I miss talking like this."

"Me too."

"I meant *talk* talk though," she said.

"I know you did. What's there to say really? It stinks."

"You'll see him again," Pal said, "and anyway, I'm not talking about Marty. I'm talking about the thing you didn't want to talk about before."

I uncrumpled the letter and read it to her.

40. DEAR JENNY,

First, last, always: I love you. Now: Please forgive me.

Maybe if I could just sleep a little I'd wake up tomorrow and this feeling will have passed. I have reason to believe it would. The feeling comes on suddenly, usually. It comes and goes. Sometimes in a day, or an hour, sometimes in a week. A month. The last month, I just can't shake it. Medication, therapy—I'm trained to know these things can save lives, and I believe in them. Just not now.

Maybe if I'd brought my guitar. Maybe then I could disappear for a while and come back whole. Or maybe I've forgotten the chords.

I can't beat it, Jenny. I close my eyes and I see it. I can't sleep and I'm afraid to be awake. After witnessing the things people do to each other, the things they don't do, I'm no good anymore.

Maybe I've been lying to you since we met, I realize only now. Lying to myself from before that even, lying forever really. I papered over it so well I fooled myself, I guess, and I've forgotten that my true color is blue.

Yes, I've seen too many bad things, and they'll only keep coming back.

That man running toward me, screaming help me, help me, except he's too bulky under his shirt. He's wired up to smoke the whole platoon. I had to shoot him.

I had to, I know I did.

I can't let that seep into you or Pop. I can't let it get into Lorenzo most of all. He deserves a chance to dream big, to dream clean. I don't trust myself to be able to hide my sadness anymore. My rage.

See, Jenny, the thing of it is, Hana died today on the way to the clinic. No, she didn't die. She was murdered, by a sniper. He shot her dead square, in the heart. And you know, after donating all that blood, she didn't get a chance to receive any herself. She bled out before we could get to her.

Hana was a teacher before they started burning down the schools. Her husband worked at an auto repair he owned. They had two girls, one a future soccer star and the other headed for science teaching, she said.

Her girls, her husband, her home, her life—all burned, all ash and fragments. And yet, somehow, Hana kept going, living in a camp, teaching the kids who sheltered there.

Now here's the kicker: The blood Hana donated in the past, on at least one occasion, ended up in the veins of her murderers. We found a wounded enemy combatant bleeding out in the middle of a firefight, and we rescued and stabilized him. Without that blood transfusion from Hana, he'd have died. He wasn't thankful. He tried to choke one of the doctors. I told Hana about it. I said maybe we should have let that sumbuck die. You know what she said? "Thank you for saving him. We all come from the same mother."

And now she's gone.

The death of an angel.

I don't get it. I do, but I don't, you know?

I'm shivering, Jenny. No warmth here. I miss

your touch too much, but I can't touch you anymore.

I love you. I love Pop. I love Lorenzo.

I'm so, so sorry,

Marty

41. PINCHING STARS

Pal had to read it again, to herself this time. And then she read it again. After a while, she said, "Renz, I'm so sad, I can't cry, you know?"

I knew all right. "It's just, how could he do that to Mom?" I said. "As he's writing the letter, he has to know that not long after, somebody in a dark green uniform is going to show up at Maple Clutch and knock on the door, and Mom's going to open it. And then she has to read *that*? He was afraid to come back. He said so himself. He was afraid to come home to us."

Pal didn't say anything. She just stroked Marty's scruff. He was watching the fire until there was the soft cracking of a stepped-on branch, and he looked over his shoulder.

A doe watched us from the dimmest part of the firelight, just into the woods. She sniffed and moved on.

"I wish he'd never written that thing," I said. "I mean, if he had to kill himself, then just do it. All that letter does is leave me wondering about him worse than I was before."

"I know," Pal said.

"You *don't* know. Your mom left you with *la gloria*. My dad left me with . . . I don't know."

"His guitar," she said. "His kindness."

"That only makes it more horrible," I said, "all the kindness he did."

"I meant *your* kindness, Renz."

Marty groinked for me to pet him.

"I don't know how to feel," I said. "That's the thing that's messing me up the most. Here he was this artist, you know? Just plain true in his music, in his medicine, taking care of the wounded. You know what? I don't want to talk about it anymore."

She nodded, and she didn't tell me it would be all right this time, and I really appreciated that.

I lay back and then Pal did the same, Marty snug between us. She was looking up at the Milky Way, so I looked up too. We were quiet for a while, until Pal said, "I heard that of all the people who ever lived, no two have the same fingerprints, including identical twins."

"What's that got to do with anything?" I said.

She was holding her hand up to the sky, pinching stars. "I don't know. I guess I was just thinking that's a little amazing is all." She looked over to me. "Don't you worry, Renz. We're gonna save Marty."

42. VIOLATORS WILL BE ~~PROSECUTED~~ SHOT

The fire died slowly, the sky slowly lightened. Pal was bunched up in her sleeping bag but her eyes were half open. "I'm awake," she said.

"I hope so," I said. "Otherwise you'd be sleeping with your eyes half open."

We had to shake Marty awake. He woke up with his tail wagging, yawned, shook himself out and farted.

"I won't miss that part," Pal said. "Oh, my Marty-moo."

"Don't start," I said.

"I *wasn't*," she said, wiping her eyes.

The footbridge was messed up from the spring floods. Here and there patches of cement had fallen from it, leaving holes big enough for a person or even a 390-pound pig to fall through.

Marty sat at the edge of the bridge and groinked, like, *No way I'm crossing that rickety mess.* I pulled out a jar of marsh butter, which was a homemade mix of marshmallows and peanut butter. I spooned it onto the safe parts of the bridge as I crossed it, and Marty trotted right along, licking up the plops.

On the other side the old pasture was a jumble of moldy refrigerators and torn tires and worst of all signs posted on every tree, right at eye level, so they would be impossible to miss:

PRIVATE PROPERTY.
NO DUMPING.
NO HUNTING.
NO TRESPASSING.
VIOLATORS WILL BE ~~PROSECUTED~~. SHOT

We leaned in closer to see the small print:

OWNER: MASON REALTY

"Figures," I said.

"He owns every acre from here to Pittsburgh by now, I bet you," Pal said.

"Maybe you need to wait here," I said.

"Oh, you mean the big strong man doesn't think the helpless little woman can survive this last stretch of the battle?"

"Fine, then you take him the rest of the way and I'll wait

here. They probably have security guards patrolling."

"Not likely," Pal said. "What's there to steal except broken washing machines and burned cars? They're just trying to scare people enough to keep them from dumping their junk here, and look how well that's worked. Renz, he's my friend too. The longer we stand here arguing, the more likely we get caught. It's less than a mile. Good quick walk, we're at the sanctuary gate in fifteen minutes. C'mon, Marty." She went and he followed.

The breeze had stopped and the air felt dead, no bird sounds either, no cicadas. We were maybe three-quarters of the way through the field when Pal said, "So far so good."

"Keep going," I said. "Come on, Marty. No time for a pee break."

But he wouldn't budge. He kept his leg lifted for a solid minute. "Okay, bud, enough." I toed him to get a move on. The weed trees broke into a clearing, and the sanctuary fence was in sight, fifty yards away—less.

"I can't believe we made it," I said.

"We didn't," Pal said. She was looking over my shoulder, pointing at something behind me, and she was pale. I turned around to look at what had her so upset, and there he was.

43. KEETH

I'd never seen a dog so big. He looked like an animal from one of those history shows about the Ice Age. He couldn't have been the father of Bella's pups. They would've been twice as big by the time we sold them off.

He stood on top of a neat high pile of old refrigerators, like somebody had stacked them to make a viewing platform for a security guard. But there was no human to restrain the dog. He was so still, I thought he was a cardboard cutout at first, the canine version of a scarecrow.

Pal zoomed in on him with her phone. "He's got the gold stripe on his head, just like Mason said. It's Keeth for sure."

The old horse farm was in the dead center of the county, in the middle of all the plots Mason had bought up over the years. I remembered from the model in his office that he planned to build his mansion here. This was the prime spot of his future kingdom. It figured he would keep his best dog here. His worst dog.

"Back away toward the fence," I said. "Pal? Slowly."

"I'm not rushing, trust me. I'm lucky if I can get myself to move. I swear I'm about to pee my pants."

"Me too, if it makes you feel any better."

"It doesn't," she said.

Marty thought we were playing a game, backing away in slow motion. He tried to push a stick into my hand to play fetch.

"Marty, stop, bud," I said. "*Marty*, no."

"Oh man, he's pacing now," Pal said.

"Don't run," I said. "It's the worst thing you could do."

"Okay I won't, I swear." Then she screamed, "Run!" and took off for the sanctuary fence.

I didn't understand why she bolted, because Keeth was still up on the platform, but then I saw it coming from the high grass—another of Mason's shepherds.

It was smaller than Keeth, but that didn't make it any less scary. Its muzzle was pulled back off its teeth, its eyes opened too wide. It was streaking right at us and faster than the fastest of the dogs who'd raced at the cinco de mayo.

"Marty, go get Pal!" I kicked him to get him going. He sprinted after Pal, and I sprinted after him. I tried to anyway.

The dog's teeth sank into the heel of my sneaker. I tripped face-first into a gravelly patch of dirt. I kicked and kicked and the dog kept biting my sneakers until I had to draw back my feet. The dog reared up and pounced for my face.

The teeth were bared, and then the jaws opened wide—and then, in a blink, he was gone.

Marty broadsided the dog, and boy was that pig mad. He outweighed the dog four to one, and he tried to bite at the dog's neck.

What the dog gave up to Marty in weight, he more than made up for with speed. He bit quicker than I thought possible, almost like I was watching life in fast forward. He got in bites all over Marty's flanks, and the blood was everywhere on him.

I kicked at the dog's back legs, but this was useless. He was so fast, he could duck me and tear into Marty at the same time.

Marty kept fighting, but he was losing so badly, just a mess of bites, and when the dog bit his back leg, Marty buckled and rolled onto his side.

The dog ripped into his belly.

Pal came with a sharp piece of rubble—a piece of cracked bathroom sink it ended up being—and swung down onto the dog's back. It let out a yip and went at Pal, but she'd hurt him. He kept spinning on himself to lick the spot down his back where she'd hit him. I picked up that piece of broken sink and swung down on his snout with it, and that was enough for him. That poor dog took off whimpering.

"Oh, no," Pal said, and the tears were coming down so hard, they ran tracks through the dust on her face and dripped mud onto her shirt. Again she pointed to something behind me.

I didn't even turn around. I just hoped he'd take me down in one deep bite to my neck so I wouldn't feel myself dying.

This close up to him, I knew for sure that Keeth was the biggest German shepherd ever born. He brushed against my leg and sniffed at Marty's blood on my jeans. He looked into my eyes, and then he turned to Marty.

He lowered his muzzle to the holes in Marty's belly and sniffed Marty's wounds.

"Renz, he's trembling," Pal said.

"I know."

"No, I mean *Keeth*," she said. "He's scared for Marty. He's whimpering. You hear him?"

That giant sweetheart of a dog, the supposed terror of the county, went down on his belly and put his head next to Marty's and licked Marty's ear to clean it.

Marty liked that. He wagged his tail. He was squealing softly. The blood trickled over the light brown coat of his underbelly.

Pal and I tore a plastic tarp from where it was tied over a stack of concrete blocks. We rolled Marty onto the plastic and dragged him toward the fence. Keeth kept licking at him until I said, "Keeth, no. Sit, boy."

He sat right down and stayed, and he shivered and whimpered as we dragged Marty away.

44. HEAVENLY HILLS

He would have been better off if I let him go to the petting zoo," I said.

"Renz, shut up about that now," Pal said. "Just let's get him to the fence."

We dragged Marty to the chain-link. It was a lot higher than it looked when we were fifty yards away. Pal climbed over it to get help while I stayed back with Marty.

"Marty?"

He wagged his tail.

"You're gonna make it, boy. I'm not going anywhere, okay? You and me, Marty. Everything's gonna be all right."

He licked my face. He tried to get up but couldn't. I hushed and soothed him, and after a while he quieted down, and his breathing slowed. His tail never stopped flicking.

The longest twenty minutes later Pal was back with a woman and a man riding a shiny new tractor mower. They came through the fence at a gate break a couple hundred yards down from where Marty and I waited. By the looks on their faces, Pal had definitely told them it was bad, but not *this* bad. The closer they came to us, their expressions went from worry to *He's a goner.*

We dragged him up the tractor bed ramp. Pal and I whispered to him on the ride to the sanctuary's veterinary clinic.

The doctor was waiting for us outside. She looked like she'd been woken up. It wasn't even seven in the morning. She checked Marty's belly and frowned.

They asked Pal and me to sit in the waiting room while they got Marty set up for surgery. Pal held my hand and kept squeezing it. "He'll be okay," she said.

"Yeah. Looked pretty bad, though, huh?" I said.

She didn't say anything.

"That was crazy about Keeth," I said.

"Sheesh, tell me about it," she said.

"It just doesn't match up," I said. "He was gentler than a puppy. How'd he get such a bad rep?"

"Right?" Pal said. "The world's upside down today."

"Why do people do that anyway?" I said. "Make up stories about how mean he is? It ruins everything."

"*Everything,*" Pal said. "What do you mean?"

"I mean he probably has no friends because of it, all the lying about him. No human friends anyway."

"I know," Pal said.

"He'll be okay," I said. "Marty, I mean."

"He'll be *fine*," Pal said, "just you wait and see."

"Yeah."

I reached into my backpack for my water bottle, and I found Marty's old tennis ball, the one he used to bounce and catch, bounce and catch, bounce and catch. I'd planned on leaving it here with him.

I squeezed it tight.

The veterinarian came out into the waiting room. "Lorenzo, come on in here for a minute," she said.

Pal and I went in. Marty was on the exam table on his side, and he was blinking kind of vacantly. He was semi-sedated, but when he saw me his tail spun a little.

The veterinarian, Doctor Esposito, put the stethoscope into my ears and put the bell end to Marty's chest.

"What is that?" I said. It was a high-pitched gurgling noise.

"He broke a rib and it nicked his lung," she said. "There's blood in it. Lorenzo, it's not likely he'll make it. Not likely at all."

Pal and I petted him while the doctor showed us how deep Marty's wounds went, and how there were too many of them.

"You went far out of your way to get him here, didn't you?" Doctor E said.

He was my teacher, I wanted to tell her. He taught me that the chance to look after somebody is a gift. Maybe Marty did imprint on me. Maybe I imprinted on him. I don't know if that's even the right thing to call it. It was a promise, just plain true, the kind where you'd risk your lives to take care of each other.

But I didn't say any of that.

"He was my friend," was all I said.

"I'm going to anesthetize him for surgery now," Doctor E said. "I wanted you to have a chance to say anything you needed to say to him." She stepped back to help her assistant get the anesthesia machine ready.

I whispered into his ear, "You're my hero, Marty. Thank you for saving me."

They shaved a patch of his leg and slipped the needle in. Not long after, his breathing slowed. He stopped blinking, and his eyes looked dull.

I read that Army medics trained themselves to be calm when death came knocking. I forced myself not to lose it. I kept my shaking inside, except there was never any hiding how I felt from Marty. He always could read me better than I could read myself. I stroked his muzzle and said, "It's okay, Marty. It's all right." Then I said to the veterinarian, "He can't hear me anymore, can he?"

"You just keep whispering to him for a little while," she said. So that's what Pal and I did.

I pushed through the clinic door into the parking lot and the dusty morning light, and there were Mom and Mr.

Lee. They were leaning back against Mr. Lee's cruiser, arms folded and frowning. But when Mr. Lee saw Pal, he spread his arms, and she ran to him.

Mom walked across the lot toward me. She walked fast, hard, almost a charge really, and she was glaring at me. She reared back with her right arm and then swung it around me and pulled me in close and told me she loved me. She was strong from working the orchard all her life, and she hugged me so tight, I ached a little. So, I guess that much was good.

PART 4

The Glory

Dear Dad,

I told my counselor about that first letter I
wrote you, the one where I said you were my hero,
the one I ripped up. Mrs. Perez said I should write
you again, that maybe it would feel different this
time. It does, even if it doesn't seem any less crazy,
writing a letter I can't send anywhere, writing to
you like you're still overseas.

That first letter, I was writing somebody I didn't
really know. But now I know you better, a little
anyway, and I have something I need to tell you.

When you wrote that playing music felt like
surfing? I guess that's how writing feels for me.
Writing things down helps me slow everything down.
I'm still trying to figure it all out, the last nine
months since that day I read your suicide note.

Dad, I know you fought the hardest you could.
You may have had the rain in your eyes, but you
were sunshine too. I'm not saying the anger isn't still
there in me, here in me. Maybe it always will be,
except mostly I feel it melting away to sadness. You

missed out, Dad. And I did too. You could have been my world. Now you're with the stars. I look up and wonder about you.

I think back to what Pal said, that no two people have the same fingerprints. I guess that means everybody's special after all. But Dad? You were really special. Thank you for writing those letters to me. Thank you for leaving me with bits of you, your guitar, your music. I wear your Bronze Star around my neck, hidden under my shirt, so it rests over my heart.

Now that I think about it, writing you feels a little less crazy. Somehow, someway, you are still around. You're here. You're in my heart. You can believe in angels now, Dad. They're real. I'm sure of it.

Love,
Renzo

Today was the first day of June, and we might as well have hopped into the broiler. Loretta, Bella and I rode in the bed of Mom's truck for the highway breeze. Loretta made the volleyball team at long last, as the assistant manager, and she had a habit of roping me in to help keep score.

We dropped her off at her house, and she gave me a

sweaty knuckle bump. "Text me when you get home," she said. Yup, I finally caved and got a stupid smartphone. I checked my text stream as Mom pulled back onto the highway. *It's a pit bull,* I texted Pal. She wanted to know about Richie Calvo's new rescue, Crusher, basically a jaw with legs, but he gave Bella a run for the sweetest dog alive.

Miss Paloma Lee was kicking some serious butt up at the Pittsburgh Professional Children's School. She'd landed a part in the Christmas musical at the Civic Light Opera. I went up there to see her. Pal was the same awesome Pal, letting herself get lost in the music. Mr. Lee took us out to a fancy dinner after. He'd found a job managing security at a hospital near Pal's school, and now, instead of a gun, he wore a tie.

I don't think I'll ever be able to make myself stop missing my good old Pal. Still, seventh grade ended up stinking a lot less than I thought it would without her. I joined this huge band called Vitamin B Cool. I know, most uncool name ever, and when I say huge, I mean we had sixteen people in the band. That's almost as many Facebook likes as we had. We ended up doing the open mike at the cinco de mayo. I wasn't as nervous this time. I wasn't as excited either, without Pal up there.

I still dream about Maple Clutch, coasting through the orchard on Buck with Marty and Bell in the trailer, or walking the pasture with them in the morning, watching the mist rise from the grass. Mason honored his word, though. He gave us a good price and a discount on one of the apartments he made out of the old motel over by the train tracks there, right in the middle of town. It was nothing fancy, but very clean. The pool was nice too. Double called it progress. I didn't know what to call it. I missed the quiet and wide openness.

Double got a part-time job working the candy counter at the train station. He loved gabbing with the travelers and telling them the five ways they could get to the riverbank café. You'd find Mrs. B visiting the candy counter from time to time too.

When Mrs. McGrath retired from being church secretary, Mom took over. The church finances were well in order, and there was definitely no robbing Peter to pay Paul. She took her lunch break in the chapel, and sometimes I'd meet her there. She'd tell me stories about my dad. There was no hiding anything now. She still loves him, she told me. She always will, she says.

The truck turned off the highway toward Heavenly Hills.

I volunteer there now. I heard about this Army veterinarian program where, if I get in, they'll pay for me to go to college. I'd get to take care of military families' pets and go on humanitarian missions to places like Ecuador and Mongolia, to fight animal-borne diseases with new vaccines. Maybe I'd even wind up taking care of the Army's working dogs, the ones that go into battle with the platoons.

Mom dropped Bell and me off at the sanctuary just in time for the dinner feeding. We got a lot of dogs, most of them abused, and I helped them remember we're not all messed up, we humans, not all the time anyway. I loved the horses too. Their eyes were so big, you could see yourself reflected in them very clearly, and you couldn't help but notice you were always smiling, crooked teeth and all.

I gave Mr. Pun'kins a scratch and went out back to romp with the pups, and there he was, smack in the middle of the roughhousing, of course:

The four-hundred-pound pig who thought he was a dog.

Turned out Mr. Pun'kins took a shine to Marty after all, and now, in addition to having a housecat, Heavenly Hills had a housepig.

I saw him twice a week, more than that if I could get a ride to the sanctuary. Each time I went out back to the corral my stomach burned a little. I worried he'd be mad at me from the last time I visited, the last time I said good-bye and hugged him and then headed fast for the door. He'd try to block me. He'd hold the cuff of my jeans in his teeth to stop me, and he'd lean into my leg and wag his tail and look up at me with those gold-brown eyes. I imagined he was thinking the same thing I was: *Why? Why can't you stay with me?*

Doctor Esposito said Marty would go to the window and

watch me until I was gone, and then he'd mope to the corner and sink to the floor and sigh and squeal quietly. Only when Mr. Pun'kins would cuddle into him would his tail start wagging again.

I called out to him, "Marty-moo!"

He was playing tug-of-war with three pit bulls over a length of rope as thick as my arm. At the sound of my voice he dropped the rope, and those three pitties went flying backward. Marty turned to me and cocked his head. His tail whirled, and he came running. He was scarred up from all the surgery they did to save him, and he limped a little, but that didn't slow him down much.

He buried his head into my armpit and oinked and trembled and licked me like he hadn't seen me in years.

The heat was still high. Bella hung back in the tree shade with the other dogs, but Marty was game for a little trip through the woods.

I led him through the meadowland to our favorite spot, the top of a great rolling hill. The sun was behind me and the grass was a little wet from an early afternoon rain, and that's when I saw it, a halo around my shadow's head, my glory.

The sky was blue like God dumped a bucket of sapphires into it. The pasture was greener than a green M&M. All I was missing was that cherry-red surfboard, and anyway my sneakers were red. Those Chuck T's might have been secondhand from the Goodwill, but they were the color of desire. I don't mind broke-in soles at all.

I'd like to visit California someday, but I don't need to anymore. I touch my heart where the Bronze Star protects it, and I feel my father with me. He was a hero all right, and so was Hana, and they are and always will be.

And Double's a hero too, and Mr. Lee and Doctor Esposito.

And Pal and Loretta.

And Richie and Mason and in a way the Taylors.

And Mrs. McGrath and Mrs. Carmela.

And Mrs. B and Mr. Santorocco, and my old teacher Mr. G, who got me thinking about heroes in the first place.

And most of all, Mom.

And maybe even me.

Heroes are everywhere.

"Marty, let's . . . *go*."

We're racing down that hill. We're slipping in spots, and in others we're sliding, but mostly we're flying. Tell you what, I am hollering. I'm like, "WooHoooooo! Bom-ba-bom-ba-bom, *bom*-ba-bom-ba-bom, *bom*-ba-bom-ba-bom-*bom*, doot-doot-*doo*."

ACKNOWLEDGMENTS

Thank you, Sarah and John for transcribing the songs. Bridget LeRoy, Eric, Bing and Georgia for letting me hang out with Fluffy and Pepper. Vincent Moustache, Maria, Jessica, Dani, Mary Kate for the beautiful cover.

Kath, MK, Leeni.

Sheila, Colleen, JD, Steve, Nicole, Ev and Doni. Andrea C., Mary R., Rebecca, Orli, Nicole M., Jennifer and Jodie.

Kim, Draga, Helen.

Carmela, Venessa, Lex, Rachel, Meriam, Kathryn.

Eileen, Dana, Julia and Kristin.

Penny, Michael, Elizabeth, Stefanie, Alaina and Text.

Jodi, Alec and Cecilia.

Jenn D and Jen L.

Regina, Jasmin, Namrata, Ellen and Lauri (with cookies for Ron Swanson).

Risa and Annie, I love you.

Kate, for being the most generous editor, teacher and friend. You're my hero.

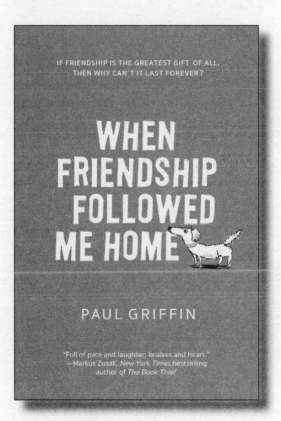

1
CHUNKY MOLD

You'd have to be nuts to trust a magician. I learned that lesson the hard way. And then, if you can believe it, I actually became a magician's assistant. That part was the Rainbow Girl's fault, but the rest of it I blame on a little dog named Flip.

The trouble started the second Friday of seventh grade. Damon Rayburn shoved me out of the lunch line. "Thanks, Coffin," he said.

"For what?" I said.

"Offering to buy me a slice."

If you think a little threat like that could get me to surrender my pizza money to an idiot like Damon Rayburn, you know me pretty well. He slapped the back of my head and cut to the front of the line.

"You're half a foot taller than him, Coffin," this kid half a foot shorter than Rayburn said. His name was Chucky Mull, but everybody called him Chunky Mold. "You should have belted him. Now he knows he can push you around."

"Allow me to quote Yoda, from *The Empire Strikes Back*," I said. "'A Jedi uses the Force for knowledge and defense, never for attack.'"

"You were being called upon to defend your inalienable right to eat meatball pizza," Mold said. "Yoda also says don't be a wimp."

"Yoda never uses the word *wimp*."

"He says, 'Fear is the path to the dark side.' Dude, hello, *The Phantom Menace*?"

There was no debating Mold on this stuff. He had the T-shirts—the sheets too. I shoved him toward our spot far, far away in the dark corner where they kept the garbage dumpster nobody ever dumped. Mold's mom had stuck a note on the waxed paper that barely covered his foot-long hero. It said, LOVE YOU. ☺ He tossed the note and crammed a hunk of sandwich into his mouth. "Any chance you would consider splitting that with me?" I said. "Come on, Mold, you'll never be able to finish the whole thing."

"Watch me," Chucky said. "Holy crud, here she comes."

Mrs. Pinto worked her way toward us. She was really pretty for a principal or even a normal human being. "Hi guys," she said.

"Good, how are you?" Mold said.

"If you ever need anything, stop by my office, okay?"

"You too," Mold said.

Mrs. Pinto patted my shoulder as she left.

"She totally just touched you," Chucky said. "You, a loser,

caressed on your loser shoulder by Mrs. P. I sent her the wink almost like four hours ago now. Nothing. Why are you staring at me like that? Dude, the emoticon? Are you visiting from The Stone Age?"

"I know what the wink is. I just can't believe you sent her one."

"So?"

"She's old. Mold, she's like *thirty*."

"It's not what you think. On Facebook the wink is a sign of supreme respect. It's like when somebody inspires you, you wink at them. It's true. It's an ancient custom that goes all the way back to classical times, the Greeks and Romanians. It's like you're bowing to her to acknowledge her awesomeness."

"Then why not just send her a bow?"

"Because there's no emoticon for that, you moron. Just because she has a totally amazing butt doesn't mean she can't be my hero too, for her, you know, incredible wisdom and everything."

"*That's* why you winked at her—her *wis*dom."

"What do you know anyway? You're not even on Facebook. It's a real thing, I swear. In many cultures it's considered rude *not* to send the wink." He batted away a fly from where the peanut butter slimed his lip like a gluey booger.

I had to believe him, firstly because you can tell when somebody's lying, and he truly didn't think he was, and most of all because he was right about me not being on Facebook. The whole *friends* thing: It wasn't really happening. Even Mold was more aggravation than ally. I moved to the neighborhood less than two years before. In a year me and my mom were heading to Florida, right after she retired. We could live great down there for cheap, she said. I figured why bother making friends when I was out of here pretty soon?

"Chucky, not even a bite? Really?" I said.

"Dream on," he said, or something like that. I couldn't tell with the sandwich all gunked up in his braces.

2

HEIR TO THE EMPIRE

My stomach was growling by the time the last bell rang and they set us free for the weekend. I headed down the board-walk toward the library. Mrs. Lorentz always kept a plate of Chips Ahoy! at the front desk.

I was feeling pretty terrific for somebody who got robbed of his pizza money. You can't be sad in Coney Island on a clear September day. The ocean was glittery. The air smelled salty and sweet. My audiobook was nearing the climax. I couldn't get caught walking around with a *book* book, of course. That's like begging for a wedgie. I cranked up my headphones and *Heir to the Empire,* by Timothy Zahn. Things were looking crummy for Han Solo. Thrawn's fighters swarmed the *Millennium Falcon.* The sound cut out when somebody came up behind me and ripped the headphones off my head.

"Who buys yellow headphones?" this girl Angelina Caramello said. She was really pretty even though she was friends with Damon Rayburn. "It's like lemons growing out of your ears."

"Plus you missed a belt loop," Angelina's best friend Ronda Glomski said. She yanked on the loop I missed. "I truly don't understand how you got skipped a grade. How can you be so lame yet so totally adorbs?"

"Ew," Angelina said. She chucked my headphones at me. Then Ronda shoved me so hard she knocked the gum out of my mouth.

I had to think about this. Ronda Glomski, ranked eleventh prettiest in our grade, said that I, Ben Coffin, was not totally revolting. Even though she practically decked me right after she said it and her name was a little gross sounding. I know, like I should talk when my name reminds you of where a zombie escaped from. We were kind of perfect for each other if you took out the part about Ronda being really mean.

In my side vision I saw Damon Rayburn coming, which meant I had to be going, and fast.

I was wheezing a little by the time I got to the library. It wasn't that far a sprint, but my asthma was kicking in, and I had forgotten my inhaler. Fortunately Mrs. Lorentz had it. "You left it on the windowsill again," she said. She pushed a book at me. "I need you to read this. My daughter can't stop talking about it. I'm looking for a second opinion before I put it on top of my stack."

It was *Feathers*, by Jacqueline Woodson. "This doesn't look like sci-fi," I said.

"You won't spontaneously combust," Mrs. Lorentz said. "Ben, you'll love it, trust me."

"After you just said you haven't read it?"

"Why are you standing here talking to me when you should be reading?"

"It's written by a girl," I said.

"So?"

"Like, I'm a dude."

"Take some cookies with you, *dude*. And yes, you can keep the fire escape door open a crack."

She let me do that on asthma days. The breeze felt nice. I didn't know it just then, but getting stopped by Angelina and Ronda, which led to me getting chased by Rayburn, which got my asthma going, which made me crack the alley door, was about to flip my life upside down.

I propped open the door with one of the grimy old encyclopedias Mrs. Lorentz was always trying to dump on everybody—Volume 10, Gargantuan to Halitosis—and settled in at my table hidden away in the back. There were all these giant pictures silkscreened onto the walls, photographs from the old days when Coney Island was the most famous beach in America. My favorite was called *Dreamland at Night*. It was the way Luna Park, this amusement park right on the ocean, looked in 1905. The tower shined like a softer sun. Think of honey lit up with the kind of electricity inside an angel's mind when she's wishing only the most beautiful things for you.

I took a breath from my inhaler and eyed *Feathers*. The cover was a picture of, guess what, a feather. No spaceships, no exploding Death Star, not even a freaking laser sword. The story went like this: There's this new kid in school. Some call him the Jesus Boy, others think he's a freak and they bully him bad. I related to him. I'm not talking about the bullying but about how I always felt like a stranger, even to myself sometimes. I just didn't know where I fit in or what I was supposed to do or be in life, like maybe I was a mistake.

Pretty soon I was on the last page of the book. The story was the kind that ends too quick and leaves you worrying about what's going to happen to the characters, almost like they're your friends, except not annoying. Frannie, the narrator, wants to be a writer. Her teacher is telling her that each day comes with its own special moments and that Frannie had better keep an eye out for them and write them down for later. I was okay with that part. I'm sure Timothy Zahn did that kind of stuff when he was writing *Heir to the Empire*. But I had to stop when I read the next thing Frannie's teacher said about these so-called special moments. "Some of them might be perfect, filled with light and hope and laughter. Moments that stay with us forever and ever."

This was a lie. Nothing lasts forever. It's a scientific fact. Things happen and they're over and you can't get them back.

Einstein said we can travel to the future, and the astronauts proved it. They synchronized twenty clocks and took ten into space. They spent six months up there, whipping around at 17,000 miles an hour, almost five miles per *second*. When they landed, *all* the clocks in Mission Control were .007 seconds ahead of *all* the ones that went into space. You see what happened? They traveled a fraction of a second into the future. Look it up if you don't believe me. This means if you travel *really* fast, like at light speed, when you land back on Earth the clocks will be *years and years* ahead, and you've escaped far into the future. Here's the problem: Einstein used the same math to prove we can never go back to the past.

I stared into the picture of Luna Park in 1905. I would never get to be there. I'd never feel safe with all those gold and silver lights on my face. I'd never see the world from the top of the tower. I'd never believe magic was real.

A cat hissed outside the fire escape door. It charged something down the alley. Then came that creepy sound a cat makes when it's mad, like a demon possessed it.

3

THE DEMON, THE DOG
AND THE DIVA

I stepped into the alley. The cat was beating the heck out of this other, much smaller one, except the little guy was a dog.

I shooed away the cat. The dog was a shivering mess. His fur was all tarred up. His tongue stuck out the side of his mouth. His eyes were gunky and pointed out toward the sides. His tail was chomped up and bent, what I could see of it. He had it between his legs. What a shrimp he was. He weighed maybe eight pounds. He wasn't young either, with the gray in his muzzle. I went to pet him. He ducked and scampered out of the alley. I tried to find him, but he was gone.

I brought *Feathers* back to Mrs. Lorentz. "So?" she said.

"It makes me upset."

"That's great," she said.

"*Great?*"

"Why does it upset you, Ben?"

"I'm not sure. Can you hold it for me?"

"You don't want to take it home?" she said.

"I forgot my backpack today."

"It weighs four point five ounces, not to mention its title is *Feathers*. You can't *carry* it?"

I looked out the window. A bunch of guys were hanging out by the free newspaper boxes everybody throws garbage in. They'd take *Feathers* and rip it up, and then Frannie and the Jesus Boy would be in pieces, getting kicked around in the wind. "How do you know it weighs four point five ounces?" I said.

"I'm guessing." She dropped the book onto a postage scale: 4.5 exactly.

"You're not human," I said.

She nodded and leaned in and whispered, "I'm a librarian." She wrote on a sticky paper and stuck it to the book. Then the weirdest thing happened. Her lips trembled and I swear she was about to cry. "Don't forget your inhaler," she said as she put the book aside to help this other kid check out a stack of video games. I leaned over the counter to see what she wrote. The note said: HOLD FOR MY BEN.

I was going to miss her next year, when Mom and I moved to Miami. It almost made me want to join Facebook, the idea that if I didn't, I'd never see her again. I would send her the biggest wink, Mrs. Lorentz, to acknowledge all the kindness she showed me the past two years, not to mention her totally amazing wisdom. I'd send her the wink every freaking day.

I was heading out when this girl was coming in. I held the door for her. She wore a lime-green beret, oversized sunglasses, a glittery scarf, and a red suit jacket with gold buttons buttoned up to her neck, even though it was like seventy-five degrees out. She wore purple gloves with the fingers cut off. Her high-tops were pink sparkles. She pretty much had every color of the rainbow covered. Her backpack was one of those mesh ones so she could show you how totally brilliant she was with all the books she had in there.

The big bad tough guys outside didn't mess with her—no sir. She was the kind of girl who, if you cracked some lame comment about her books or *gloves* or whatever, she'd come back with something that made you feel even stupider than you are, and in front of all your buddies too. Even the dumbest guy knows not to mess with a diva.

And boy, was she one. She stopped to check a text. Here I am, holding the freaking door for her, and the whole time she's texting back. And then she brushed right past me without even tossing me a thanks.

"You're *wel*come," I said. No I didn't. I just left.

It was five thirty. Mom liked me home by six to help with dinner. The tide was coming in. The salt smell was strong enough to make you cough. Papers blew around the street. I had a feeling I was being followed.

I turned around. Mermaid Avenue was packed with everybody coming home from work, but nobody seemed interested in me. I headed up to Neptune, which was a little less crowded, and now I was sure somebody was stalking me. I spun around, and there he was.